Totally Bound Publishing books by Bella Settarra

The Cowboys of Cavern County
Carla's Cowboys
Maggie's Man
Two for Trinity
Isla's Irish Cowboy

I0658940

The Cowboys of Cavern County

SAVANNAH'S SAVIORS

BELLA SETTARRA

Savannah's Saviors
ISBN # 978-1-78686-375-1
©Copyright Bella Settarra 2018
Cover Art by Emmy@studioenp ©Copyright October 2018
Interior text design by Claire Siemaszkiewicz
Totally Bound Publishing

SAVANNAH'S SAVIORS

Dedication

To Heidi.
Thank you for all your support and for loving my
cowboys as much as their heroines and I do. xx

Chapter One

The cruel rain pelted her like bullets as Savannah trudged through the muddy track that led her deeper into the back of beyond. Too exhausted to cry now, she muttered to herself about the injustice of it all, occasionally shouting into the looming darkness, imagining she was yelling at Daniel – as if she'd ever have the nerve.

Maybe that was what made it all the more galling, the fact that she'd never plucked up the courage to do anything about the way she had been treated – the way he had *mis*treated her for the past three years. But Daniel Edgerton was a clever man. Too clever. He'd say things that hurt her, belittled her, angered her even, but there had been nothing she could do about it. If she sulked, he'd ignore her. If she cried, he'd ask what on earth the matter was. And if she shouted? Well, no one could shout louder than him.

She hadn't shouted tonight, though. It had barely been a whisper when she had told him she wanted a divorce. It made sense, in her head. Neither of them was happy and there was no reason to prolong the agony. But he hadn't seen it the same way. Daniel always had his own way of looking at things.

"Of course we're happy," he told her in astonishment, his thin lips curled into an ugly sneer. "What are you talking about, woman?"

"But I don't please you and you always shout at me," she murmured, clearing away his still-half-full supper plate. "The meals I cook are never right, the clothes I wear are all wrong and you always complain about how I wear my hair."

"Then learn to cook. Wear what I tell you and stop tying your hair up like an old crone." His lips were tight with anger.

She sighed, his last comment cutting her deep. "I don't think there's anything wrong with my cooking. If you do, then maybe you should let me attend the cooking classes in the Town Hall, like I suggested last month. The clothes you want me to wear are too tight and too short for decency. And I tie my hair back while I'm working in the house to keep it tidy and out of the way."

"So, you think you're perfect?" he jeered, running a stiff hand through his sandy hair.

"No. Neither of us is perfect," she said. 'But I can see that I don't make you happy, so I want us to get a divorce."

"You don't want me?" he accused her, narrowing his icy-gray eyes.

"No more than you want me, if you're honest, Daniel." She hoped to appeal to his logical side, the one he used every day at work. By laying it all out plainly, maybe they could discuss the matter like the adults they were — sensible, compromising adults.

"Then you don't want anything from me? You don't want my house or my money?"

Her stomach thudded. "Daniel, I'm not after your money. You know that. I've never been after your money." Tucking *a stray of wavy, red hair behind her ear, she stared at him beseechingly.*

"Good." He stood up then, walked over and opened the front door. The wind had blown in a torrent of rain. "Go on, then. Out."

She stared at him. "I didn't mean tonight. I haven't packed yet, as you're well-aware. And I haven't made any plans. I thought we'd just talk about it first, decide…"

"You've already decided." His voice was deep and booming out at her, making her quiver.

"Daniel, I — "

"Now. And don't even think of taking anything with you. Everything in this house has been bought with my money — not yours. As you don't want my money, that won't be a problem, will it?"

"But — "

"Out!"

She walked toward the door, shaking with cold as well as fear. His face was stiff, his lips nothing more than a thin line and his steely eyes had faded with fury. There would be no reasoning with him.

"And you can forget about a divorce!" he yelled after her as she crossed the threshold.

Even the howling wind couldn't drown out the slam of the door as soon as she went through it, and she took a deep breath, determined not to crumble, not to give him what he wanted…for once.

That same wind had mocked her all night and the rain had long since soaked her to the skin. Her jeans stuck to her legs like leeches, and her woolen sweater had stretched out of shape and hung around her icy flesh.

Her torn sneakers sloshed in the marshy embankment, and she stepped out into the track to avoid a huge puddle.

Suddenly, two lights split the night and she turned just in time to see a large vehicle veer to the left. She spun around to climb the slope, out of its way, but her foot slid on the wet mud and she screamed as she hit the ground.

"There's someone here," somebody cried out.

There was a panicked shout and moments later a flashlight shone in her face, making her flinch.

"Are you okay?" A man's frantic voice permeated the mush in her head as he ran toward her, followed by someone else.

At first, she was afraid it was Daniel, having come looking for her — worried, guilty, sorry. She knew he wouldn't be happy with her, no matter how else he felt. It wasn't him, though.

With a mixture of relief and disappointment, she peered at the men who had joined her. "I'm fine," she replied.

"We just came around that bend and..." the guy behind blurted out.

"So it was *my* fault?" She'd never spoken to a stranger like that before, but she'd had enough blame to last her a lifetime.

"No, of course not. It was an accident. I thought you were an animal of some kind, and... Oh God, I'm so sorry. I..."

"Let's get you out of this mess, shall we?" the first guy offered a little more calmly, taking her arm.

"No, I don't need your — Aah!" She'd put her weight on her right foot and the pain was agonizing. She couldn't hold her balance and the guy put his other arm around her and scooped her up as though she weighed nothing.

"It's your leg, huh?" he asked. "I'm Greg, by the way. Greg Jackson. That's Tom."

Greg was already striding over the road toward their truck, carrying her carefully.

"Don't you have a bag or coat or anything?" Tom was shining his flashlight all around the area, searching for her belongings.

Both guys seemed even more shaken up than her at the accident.

"No, but…"

"Let's get you inside. You're soaked right through, sweetheart." Greg had somehow managed to open the door to the truck and the courtesy light shone down on them, showing him to be a very handsome man.

"I don't think so, thank you," she told him, trying to push back against his thick-set, muscular frame. "I'm not going anywhere with a couple of strangers."

Greg chuckled. "Well, I did tell you my name. And I've introduced you to my friend there, Tom Rankin, so the way I see it, we're not exactly strangers, although we haven't heard your name yet." His deep blue eyes twinkled while Tom wrapped a blanket around her.

The soft wool was warm and soothing against her and she closed her eyes to savor the sensation. Greg set her in the middle of the bench seat while Tom leaned in and buckled her up.

"What're you doing? I said –" Her eyes sprang open in shock as the men sat on either side of her, their welcoming warmth making her shudder.

Tom started the engine with shaking hands. "Where are you headed?" he asked her, his kind brown eyes staring into her face.

"Umm…"

"Well, you can't be from around here 'cause there aren't any houses for miles," Greg said matter-of-factly as he slammed his door shut.

The truck started to move and warm air blew toward her. She pulled the blanket tighter while her mind whirled with confusion. Greg put an arm around her. She tried to push him off but didn't have the strength.

"Could be hypothermia," he muttered, undeterred.

Savannah had stopped shivering some time ago, feeling the cold take over her whole body. She closed her eyes in the warmth of the cab, knowing she should be trying to figure a way out of here, but she was so tired and confused that she couldn't think straight. Her concern at being alone with two strange men seemed to fade into oblivion, however, as everything turned black.

* * * *

"We did the right thing," Greg assured his friend, as he climbed into bed.

"I know," Tom replied, poking his head through the doorway that led to their tiny en suite bathroom, where he was cleaning his teeth. "I'm just worried about her. She didn't sound too happy when we found her, did she?" He rinsed his mouth and returned to the twin-bedded room he shared with his buddy.

"She could have been in shock," Greg replied. "You heard what the doc said. It was a good thing we found her when we did. She already had the onset of hypothermia. If she'd been out there all night, she'd have..."

"I know," Tom cut in.

Greg sighed. He knew Tom was as worried as he was about the poor girl, and his friend felt guilty for almost running her over on that dirt track. But it wasn't his friend's fault. In fact, it was a good job he had, in a way. Had they driven on past, they might not have noticed the young waif in a dark sweater, soaked to the skin on the lonely stretch of road.

"You probably saved her life, bro," Greg told him, knowing full well how close to home his remark would be.

Tom snorted. "She only twisted her ankle."

"You know what I mean." Greg was sure Tom wouldn't want to think about it that way, but they both knew it was true. "The doc said she'd be asleep for hours yet. I think we should do the same."

"I wonder if one of us should stay with her," Tom murmured as Greg switched off the lamp.

"Nah. It's like a furnace in there. We wouldn't last five minutes. And Mrs. H is perfectly happy to look after her. You saw how she was."

Their landlady had been horrified when they'd arrived carrying the wet bundle, and she'd insisted on putting Savannah into some dry clothes while Greg called the doctor. Mrs. Hodges ran a very nice bed-and-breakfast in Pelican's Heath and was only too pleased to put the girl up in one of her spare rooms. She'd already gotten her bundled up with thick blankets and Tom had fetched the spare electric heater from the loft to ensure the room was extra-warm.

The doctor had examined the girl, diagnosing early hypothermia and a sprained ankle. There were some nasty bruises on her back, too, and a scar on her shoulder that he was going to ask her about in the morning. The bruising might have been from the fall, but he wasn't sure. He expected her to regain consciousness in a few hours, and Mrs. Hodges had insisted on staying with her until she did. After strapping her ankle, he had left painkillers and a list of instructions with the old lady before promising to be back the next day.

Although it didn't feel right, Greg knew the best thing they could do was get some sleep themselves, if at all possible. They'd had a long day at the ranch and would need all their strength.

* * * *

Savannah awoke in a warm room with a candle flickering beside the bed. Shadows danced around the walls, which she noticed were covered in pretty wallpaper with a ditsy print. A stream of light through a gap in the long drapes showed that dawn was on its way.

She frowned at a gray-haired woman who was asleep in the small armchair next to the bed. She didn't recognize her or the room. The faint scent of lavender relaxed her a little as her head whirled in bewilderment.

A jug of water sat on the neat little nightstand, reminding her how dry her throat was, and she sat up and leaned over to pour herself a drink.

"What are you doing?"

She was startled by the lady's crisp voice and yanked her hand back from the jug. Her heart pounded with surprise and she pulled the covers closer to her, drawing her knees up. A sharp pain in her right foot made her flinch.

"It's all right," the lady said, in a much softer voice, putting a hand out in a placating fashion. "My name is Mrs. Hodges and you're at my bed-and-breakfast in Pelican's Heath."

Savannah gaped at the woman.

"I'm… I'm Savannah Edgerton," she replied, her throat much croakier than she expected. "Why am I here?"

She racked her brain but could only remember walking through the darkness in driving rain, feeling numb.

"Greg and Tom found you on the back road from Almondine," Mrs. Hodges explained. "You fell and hurt your ankle."

Savannah's mind cast back to the headlights and the puddle, to the two guys who'd insisted on putting her into their truck, out of the rain. It all seemed like a dream, somehow. But what about...? Her stomach roiled as she remembered Daniel throwing her out of their home, the slamming door echoing into the night. The familiar feeling of dread engulfed her and she squeezed her eyes shut to stop tears from escaping.

"Hey, it's all right. You're safe here," Mrs. Hodges assured her, patting her hand over the bedcover. "Here... Let me get you some water."

Savannah opened her eyes and took a drink. It was cool and slid down her throat, which had now gained a large, miserable lump.

"Thank you."

"So, are you warm enough, Savannah?"

The question surprised her a little and she snuggled into the coverlet, more for comfort than warmth. "Yes, thank you."

"You got very cold last night. The doc was worried about hypothermia, so I've turned up the temperature for you. It's a little too warm for me, to be honest, but we had to make sure you were okay. You gave us all quite a fright."

Savannah raised her eyebrows. "Really? I didn't mean to. I'm so sorry."

The old lady chuckled. "Don't be sorry. We just wanted you to be okay."

"That's very kind of you. But I'm fine, honestly."

"Are you hungry? I thought I'd make myself some oatmeal with warm milk. Would you like some?"

"That would be lovely." Savannah managed a grateful smile, and Mrs. Hodges rose from her chair.

"You keep nice and cozy. It won't take long."

As the old lady left the room, Savannah snuggled down again, her head whirling with possibilities and her memory replaying that awful scene with her husband like a scratched record.

Her ankle hurt like the devil and that worried her. How was she going to get away from Daniel if she couldn't even walk? And how far had she gotten from him already? She'd heard of Pelican's Heath, on the other side of Almondine, but how far was that from Upton Crossing? She closed her eyes, wishing she could shut out all her worries with just a blink. It wasn't going to be that easy, though. It never was, not when Daniel was involved. She must have dozed, because the next thing she knew, she was awoken to a lady's voice.

"Here we are."

Mrs. Hodges had come back with a tray, and Savannah opened her eyes and slid up the bed to a sitting position.

"Should you be moving that much already?" A guy with what looked like dark hair and stubble was standing in the doorway.

Savannah jumped, her heart pounding.

"She seems to be all right," Mrs. Hodges assured him as she placed the tray beside the water on the nightstand.

He sauntered into the room and pulled back the drapes to reveal a bright orange sky. It shot a cozy glow around the room, enabling Savannah to examine her surroundings a little more fully.

The room was a peachy color, and she wasn't sure whether that was down to the sunrise or the decor. Whichever way, it made for a calming atmosphere. Mrs. Hodges handed her a bowl of oatmeal, which she took with both hands—that, she noticed, were trembling. Her hostess wasn't quite as elderly as she had first thought, and she guessed her to be in her early sixties. Her gray hair had clearly been set on rollers recently but now looked flattened in places. She had an austere appearance and wore a long nightgown, buttoned right to the neck.

"Here… Let me help you with that." The guy walked over to the bed and went to take the bowl from her.

"No, it's fine." Savannah almost panicked as he rounded on her.

"You're shaking. And it might be a little hot yet, anyway," he insisted, leaning even closer to her and prying the food from her hands.

Savannah was about to object when she smelled his delicious, musky cologne and looked up into the deepest chocolatey eyes she had ever seen. He stared down at her, his face growing a little red, his mouth twitching at the corners. She recognized him from the previous night but couldn't recall his name. His gaze oozed warmth and his tight jaw suggested that he was even more stubborn than she was. Okay, she'd let him have this one, but no way was she prepared to give in to him every time. She'd spent her life giving in to everyone else and look where it had gotten her. It seemed like she was on a narrow precipice, clinging on for dear life. Her only hope was to stay strong, and that was exactly what she intended to do.

The bed dipped as the guy sat down facing her, his warm eyes studying her as he stirred her breakfast.

"I think it's ready," he announced after a few moments and leaned forward again, offering her a spoonful.

Savannah wanted to tell him that she wasn't a baby, that she could manage quite well without his help, but the look on his face changed her mind. She opened her mouth and allowed him to feed her. It was worth it. The oatmeal was delicious and seemed to soothe that lump in her throat.

"I'm Tom, by the way."

"It's nice to meet you, Tom-by-the-way. I'm Savannah Edgerton."

Tom's eyes shone at her in surprise before he chuckled from deep in his throat. Then he hooted with laughter.

Mrs. Hodges giggled, too.

"I can see we're going to have our hands full with you, Savannah Edgerton," he said once he'd recovered himself.

I hope so, she thought, then immediately admonished herself. He was a great-looking guy with a sense of humor and kind eyes, but that didn't mean anything. She still wasn't out of the woods yet.

Blushing, she averted her gaze.

"Open wide," he instructed, forcing her to look his way again. *Damn him!*

She hadn't realized just how hungry she was or how much her throat hurt after all the crying she'd done last night. Tom was very patient as he offered her each spoonful and she savored the food as it slid down.

She finished the last mouthful with a mixture of relief and disappointment. She'd enjoyed having him feed her, and the oatmeal really had been delicious. Now that he'd finished his task, however, he had no reason to stay here.

And neither have I.

Chapter Two

"Where are my clothes?" Savannah asked Mrs. Hodges after Tom had left the room.

"I put them in the washer last night. They were covered in dirt, as were you. I'll fetch them for you, if you like."

"Yes, please," she said, trying to imagine what a state she must have looked when she arrived here. "Would it be okay if I took a shower, too?"

"If you can do it without getting that ankle wet," Mrs. Hodges replied, "The doctor didn't leave a spare bandage."

"I will."

"Morning." Another guy poked his head around the bedroom door, just as Mrs. Hodges was getting up from her seat.

"There you are, Greg. I wondered if you'd overslept or something," the older lady said.

"Nah. I just had an early morning call from Frankie. She wants to meet up with me and Tom at lunchtime."

He walked into the room and over to the bed. "Anyway, I wondered how our patient was doing this morning." He grinned at Savannah and her face grew hot. He was handsome, with perfect teeth gleaming from his tan face. His fair hair was quite wavy, almost collar-length, and his deep blue eyes twinkled.

"She'll live," Mrs. Hodges told him, giving Savannah a friendly wink.

"I'm fine. Thanks for looking after me — both of you."

"That's all right. Mrs. H doesn't do anything all day long, so it'll do her good to have someone to fetch and carry for today," Greg replied.

Mrs. Hodges went as if to swipe him with her hand, but he just laughed and ducked out of her way.

"Can you see what I have to put up with?" She smiled at Savannah. "Tom's just as bad. I don't know why I let them stay here so long."

"Because you love us," Greg said, blowing her a kiss. "You'll be lost when we move out."

"Any news on that?" Mrs. Hodges asked, raising her eyebrows.

"We're hoping to hear something today," Greg told her, holding up his crossed fingers.

Mrs. Hodges nodded, but Savannah noticed how disappointed she looked. She guessed Greg had been right about her missing the guys when they left.

"What do you think Frankie's after?"

"Mrs. H, she doesn't have to be *after* anything," he admonished her. "Maybe she just wants to meet up as friends." He shrugged.

Mrs. Hodges snorted before leaving the room.

Greg shook his head. "Are you sure you're okay?" He looked concerned as he turned back to Savannah.

"Yes, honestly. I'm going to get up in a minute."

"You don't have to. It's not even seven o' clock yet. Me and Tom have some extra work to do over at the ranch. We don't always start this early."

"I do," she replied.

"Where do you work?"

"I don't go out to work anymore," she told him, a little sadly. "I just have to be up before my husband so I can tend to him and clean the house."

Greg frowned. "Is he disabled?"

"No. Why would you think that?"

"But he needs a lot of help? You said you *tend* to him."

"Oh no, only in the way that any wife tends to her husband. You know…run his bath, lay out his clothes, cook his breakfast—that sort of thing."

Greg raised his eyebrows "So you're…happily married?"

She couldn't hold his gaze. He seemed like a great guy, but she could tell what he was thinking—if she was so happily married, why was she out in a storm in the middle of the night, lost and alone?

"Have you called him? Told him where you are? If you need a ride home, we can always—"

"No." She hadn't meant to sound so abrupt. "I-I mean, no, I haven't called him yet. I will once I'm washed and dressed." She offered a weak smile, glancing up at him.

He narrowed his eyes and she just knew he wasn't convinced.

"So, you might not be here when we get back later?" Greg asked.

Damn! Even if she knew where to go, she wouldn't get very far with that ankle, and she had no money for a bus.

"My husband's away, actually, so he won't be able to fetch me just yet," she said. "I'm not sure whether I'll stay here or —"

"Of course you'll stay here." Mrs. Hodges swept into the room, carrying her clothes, all neatly folded. "Where else would you go?"

Savannah sighed with relief at the old lady's timely intervention, although she wondered how long Mrs. Hodges might have been waiting outside the door, listening.

"You're very kind," she told her. "I've no money on me, but I'll send you some when I get home."

"Don't you worry about that," Mrs. Hodges said, shaking her head. "I'm glad to help."

Savannah smiled at her. "Thank you."

"So, where's home?" Greg asked.

"Um, it's quite a way, actually," she said. "The other side of Almondine."

"Does this place have a name?" Greg frowned.

"Come on, bro. We'll be late if you don't stop your gassing." Tom burst into the room at the perfect moment. He turned to Savannah with a smile. "You just can't shut him up," he explained, shaking his head. "He's just like an old w…" He stopped as he noticed Mrs. Hodges place her hands on her hips. "Well, you know what I mean," he finished with a grin.

"Out, the pair of you. I've got work to do — contrary to popular belief — even if you haven't," Mrs. Hodges said, ushering both guys out of the door.

"See you later, Savannah," Tom called back with a chuckle. "Probably around lunchtime."

* * * *

"I meant to talk to you about that," Greg said, as they climbed into the truck.

"Savannah?"

"Lunchtime."

"Oh." Tom frowned as Greg gunned the engine and they took off in the direction of the Shearer Ranch.

"Frankie called while you were taking a shower. She wants to see us around one o' clock in the diner." He peered over for Tom's reaction.

"You're kidding!"

"'Fraid not. She says it's important."

"Jeesh! How long's it been? A month? What the hell can she have to say to us now?"

"I dunno. I thought she was with what's-his-name, although it hasn't stopped her giving us the eye just lately, has it?"

"Yeah, I noticed." Tom shook his head. "If you ask me, that girl wants her bread buttered on both sides. I can't believe she cheated on us after... What? A week? Why on earth would she want to speak to us now?"

"There's only one way to find out," Greg replied, pursing his lips.

"I don't think I *want* to find out," Tom admitted. "I've got nothing to say to that girl and I really don't want to waste my time listening to anything she has to talk about. I vote we blow her off and spend some time with Savannah instead. I'd like to get to know her."

Greg raised an eyebrow in surprise. "You like her, don't you?"

"Are you saying you don't?"

"No. She's beautiful but she's off-limits, I'm afraid. She's a married woman."

Tom looked crestfallen. "*Happily* married?

"Ah, well. Therein lies the mystery."

Tom stared at him. "Just what *were* you yakking on about this morning?"

"She didn't actually say much, but I kind of got the impression it's not all rosy at home — wherever that is." He rolled his eyes, recalling his friend's untimely arrival earlier. "She told me her husband was away."

"So why was she out last night? Was she lost?"

"I didn't get time to ask her about that," Greg admitted "It sure seems strange, don't you think — her being out on her own in those conditions without a coat or bag or anything?"

"I thought that last night," Tom agreed as they pulled up on the ranch.

"You didn't get much sleep, either, huh?"

"Nope, though it's hardly surprising, is it?"

Greg nodded as they stopped.

"Hey, guys, thanks for coming in early." Matt Shearer met them near the stables. He was a real nice guy, about the same height as them at six-foot-three, with wavy hair and light stubble on his chin.

"No problem, boss. Happy to help out," Greg said with a smile.

"We've got more cattle being delivered in about a half hour," Matt said.

"The west field's all ready for them." Greg had the blisters to prove it, too. They'd spent all day yesterday working on the new fencing and a couple of days before that scouring the whole area for poisonous weeds.

"Great. Carla's got some coffee on and she said to go through and get some breakfast."

Tom's eyes lit up. "Thanks, boss."

One of the perks of working for the Shearers was their girlfriend, Carla. She was always friendly and baked cakes to go with their coffee — even cooked breakfast on days like today when they had an early start. The ranch was growing and Matt had run it single-handed for years, with just the occasional hired help when things got really busy. His twin brother Dyson was the local sheriff and only worked on the ranch when he had time. This was definitely Matt's domain.

"Good morning." Carla beamed as they entered the large kitchen. She wore jeans and a pretty blue top under a large apron, her beautiful wavy hair tied back in a loose ponytail. It wasn't hard to see what had attracted the Shearer brothers to the pretty girl.

"Hey, Carla, is that bacon I can smell?" Greg grinned, peering over her shoulder at the stove.

She nodded. "Have a seat and help yourselves to coffee, guys. I'll be with you in just a minute."

They didn't need telling twice and were soon tucking into large platefuls of bacon and eggs with pancakes and waffles.

"I can't help wondering what Frankie wants," Greg said through a mouthful of waffle. "She sure sounded cryptic on the phone."

"It's probably nothing," Tom replied with a shrug. "You know what a drama queen she is."

"Is everything all right?" Carla joined them for a coffee.

"Seems that we've been summoned by Frankie," Tom said with a grimace, "though we've got nothing to say to each other."

Carla frowned. "She's still with Jonathan Morgan, isn't she? I saw them in the shop the other day."

Tom scoffed. "Yeah, as far as we know they're still together. He pushed his plate to one side. "He obviously has something we don't."

"A large bank account, I reckon, buddy." Greg rolled his eyes. "Don't sweat it."

"I'm not," Tom said. "Thanks very much for the breakfast." He managed a smile for Carla before getting up. "I'll go wait for the delivery."

"I'll be there in a minute," Greg promised, tucking into another waffle.

The door closed behind Tom.

"He really liked her, didn't he?" Carla frowned.

"Yeah, I reckon he did. Pity she didn't feel the same way, though," Greg said with a sigh.

"How long were you guys together?"

Greg gave a self-deprecating snigger. "A week — and she even cheated on us in that time."

Carla shook her head. "That was just mean."

"I didn't realize Tom had taken it so badly, but he sure seems sore about it. I think it's more his pride that's hurt, to be honest. We only knew her a few days before we asked her out, so he hadn't had time to become really attached. I heard she'd known Jonathan much longer than that. Beats me why they didn't just get together in the first place."

Carla pursed her lips. "Jonathan Morgan only got promoted last month. He'll be getting good money now, especially working for the Fieldings." She looked a little sad. "We could never afford to pay the sort of wages they can."

"Money isn't everything," Greg reminded her. "Give me happiness over wealth any day." He smiled at her.

"Are you guys happy here?"

"We're more than happy. Matt and Dyson have given us a chance, and so have you. We couldn't ask for more than that. We love working here and we're planning to settle in Cavern County. Folks are so accepting around these parts."

She smiled. "We don't all agree with that judge's decision. Besides, everyone deserves a second chance."

"But not everyone's willing to offer one. We appreciate what you guys have done for us, and we'll pay it back in any way we can."

"I think they'll just be happy with your loyalty."

"That's a given. What you all gave us was worth a lot more than that." He wiped his mouth with a napkin and stood up. "And now, I'd better get some work done before y'all change your minds. Thanks again for the meal." He winked at her and went to join Tom outside.

"Do we really have to see Frankie today?" Tom looked thoughtful.

Greg sighed. "I can't make you out, buddy. I thought you liked the girl. How come you don't want to see her?"

Tom raised his eyebrows. "*Liked* her, past tense. I thought she was nice, quite pretty and fun to be around. Not as wonderful as Beth, of course, but Frankie was just stringing us along. She had no intention of having a ménage relationship with us. Jonathan Morgan just clicked his fingers and she came running. We didn't mean anything to her. She played us for a couple of fools."

"She's known him a while, but maybe he didn't have much to offer her. He just got promoted over at the Fielding Ranch, according to Carla."

Tom whistled. "The Fieldings? They've got to be one of the richest families around here."

Greg nodded. "They pay well, too. Jonathan'll be making good money now — which should make him quite a catch, don't you think?"

Tom pursed his lips "He's still pug-ugly, though. Unless he's planning to spend some of his pay raise on a face-lift and a new body, nothing's gonna change that."

"And a haircut... You can't forget that hair," Greg pointed out with a chuckle.

"Fuck, no. Well, at least it proves one thing. Frankie sure wasn't with us for our money, which means it must have been our looks that attracted her."

"I can live with that." Greg nodded. "Begs the question, though... What in hell does she want with us now?"

Chapter Three

Savannah was bored—confused and bored. She'd been glad to have a shower and wash her hair. It had been really stuffy in the bedroom with all the heaters and blankets, though she was grateful that she had been so well looked-after. She was a little weak but determined to carry on as though nothing had happened. As long as she could get back on her feet soon, she'd be happy, despite the constant throb of her head and her whole body feeling heavy and achy.

She'd left her long, wavy red hair loose so it would dry quicker and she was grateful that her clothes had been washed. She had managed—with some difficulty—to get downstairs, but Mrs. Hodges had insisted that she wasn't allowed to do anything except sit with her foot elevated on a soft pouf and read magazines while the older lady pottered around with a duster and the vacuum cleaner.

"It doesn't feel right watching you do all the work," Savannah had protested. "At least let me polish those silver vases or something."

"Guests don't work in my house," Mrs. Hodges had informed her, shaking her head.

"*Paying* guests, maybe, but I haven't given you a penny toward my keep yet," Savannah pointed out. "At least let me do *something* while I'm just sitting here. I hate doing nothing."

Eventually, the older lady had relented and, after stoking the fire one more time, she furnished Savannah with the silverware and some polish.

The doctor had called on her earlier and declared Savannah in much better health than he had feared the previous night. "Though it looks like a bad cold, judging by the redness of your throat and the amount of sniffing you are doing," he'd warned.

Savannah hadn't wanted to mention her sore throat, her aching head or the way her nose was constantly streaming—though the latter wasn't as easy to hide—and had just nodded and accepted the hot lemon with honey that Mrs. Hodges offered her.

She had been a little disappointed that the two guys hadn't made it back at lunchtime, as she'd have liked the distraction, though she knew it was for the best. She wasn't in a position to start making friends right now and assumed they'd decided to keep to their arrangement with Frankie, anyway.

"Is she Greg's girlfriend?" she asked Mrs. Hodges, as they sat at the kitchen table for some chicken soup with homemade bread.

"Frankie? She was with both of them—for about a week, if that."

Savannah was surprised to feel a little twinge of jealousy at the thought and admonished herself. After all, she didn't really know them, and she had to remember she was a married woman. The thought of one lucky woman getting to share *both* the handsome hunks made her stomach burn, though.

"How come?" She couldn't resist the question, although she was well aware that it was none of her business.

"I'm not really sure," Mrs. Hodges admitted. "They'd only been in town a few weeks when they asked her out. Frankie's lived around here all her life and had quite a few boyfriends, so I wasn't too surprised."

"Well, they are handsome guys." Savannah was only thinking aloud and shocked herself that the words had passed her lips.

"Oh, you noticed, huh?" Mrs. Hodges smiled.

Savannah shrugged, biting her tongue—something she wished she'd done earlier.

"They only took her out a couple of times. Then it turned out she'd dumped them to go out with Jonathan Morgan." She shook her head. "Can't see the attraction, myself."

"He's not that good-looking, then? Jonathan Morgan?"

"I suppose beauty's in the eye of the beholder," the lady replied. Then she leaned forward. "Though I figure you'd have to be *very* beholden to find him handsome."

Savannah giggled. It seemed Mrs. Hodges was much more fun than she had first imagined. "Perhaps he's rich," she offered.

"I wouldn't know," she said, scraping the last of the soup from her bowl. "He's a ranch hand over with the Fieldings."

"I don't know them."

"They're a rich family. Real nice people, too," Mrs. Hodges informed her.

"Is that the same ranch that Greg and Tom work on?"

Mrs. Hodges shook her head, her gray curls wobbling. "No. The guys work for Matt Shearer. His twin brother's the local sheriff. They've got a girlfriend, too, Carla. They're a lovely family."

Savannah frowned. "They own a ranch but one of the brothers is the sheriff? Are they rich as well, then?"

Mrs. Hodges piled up the empty dishes. "No. They took on the ranch after their parents died. Dyson suffers real bad with arthritis, though, and found all the manual labor a bit tough going, so he took the job as the local law enforcer while Matt took care of the family business. Dyson helps his brother out from time to time, but now he's been made sheriff, he's kept busy enough in town. Carla's a hard worker and she helps Matt quite a bit. The ranch is doing really well, though, and they've just been able to buy more cattle. That's why the guys had to go in a little earlier today. They were having some delivered this morning."

Savannah smiled. It was good that Mrs. Hodges took such an interest in the local community and in her guests' lives. She was clearly quite fond of Greg and Tom.

"Why don't you go in by the fire and I'll bring us some coffee?" Mrs. Hodges suggested.

Savannah was tempted to ask if she could lend a hand with the washing-up first, but the look on the older lady's face made her think twice. "Thank you. That was lovely," she said, before hobbling back into the living room. She was pleased for a chance to relax, as every limb on her body throbbed. Mrs. Hodges joined her after a few minutes.

"So, what about you?" The elderly woman handed her a hot mug and a slice of chocolate cake before taking the chair opposite her.

Savannah's heart beat a little faster and her face heated. "Me?"

"Yeah. You said you're from the other side of Almondine. That must be out Upton way or Jacobstown?"

"Upton Crossing." Savannah had no option other than to answer her, though she really didn't want to divulge anything about herself.

Mrs. Hodges nodded. "That's quite a way."

"Yes. What about you? Are you from around here originally, Mrs. Hodges?" She hoped that changing the subject might help keep the heat off herself.

"Born and bred. That's why I'm so fascinated with folks who aren't. So, what brought you to Pelican's Heath in the middle of the night?"

Savannah sighed. "I'm looking for someone," she lied.

Mrs. Hodges frowned, while Savannah's mind whirled. She hadn't thought about what she was going to tell anyone about how she came to be here. It had been naive of her to think that she could just pass through without having to explain herself, but she didn't have a clue what to say. She cursed once again for hurting her ankle. If she'd just been more careful, she would be miles away by now.

"In the middle of the night with no bags or anything?"

Damn! She knew Mrs. Hodges wouldn't leave it there.

She giggled a little nervously and took a large bite of her cake to buy herself some thinking time. "Well, when I say *someone*, I mean…I mean my dog." The story came to her in a flash of inspiration that she accredited to the chocolate cake, which was delicious.

"Your dog?" Mrs. Hodges narrowed her eyes.

"Yes, my dog Willow. We'd been out for a walk when I thought it was such a nice day we could go to the river in Almondine. I was getting tired, so we took the bus most of the way."

Mrs. Hodges nodded.

"We had a lovely time. I hadn't taken him there in ages, but as my husband was away, I thought it would be a good opportunity to spend some quality time with him, as we didn't have to hurry back or anything. Willow was jumping in and out of the water as I strolled along the riverbank then he suddenly ran off. I thought he must have smelled a rabbit or something and didn't really worry at first. I figured he'd soon come back when he realized he couldn't fit down a rabbit hole."

"Is he a big dog?"

Savannah nodded. "Yes. I'm not sure what type he is. He's a mutt. A mix of several different types, I think. We bought him from the animal shelter. Anyway, I just kept walking, hoping to find him, but then it started getting dark and I got worried. I just kept going in the general direction we'd been strolling in, praying he'd suddenly just pop up from the bushes or something. Then the weather got bad, but I didn't want to just leave him, so I kept walking. I didn't realize how late it had gotten or how far I'd gone."

"So the dog's still out there somewhere?"

"Yes." Savannah did her best to look sad.

"Maybe he'll have just gone home. Dogs do that."

"I know. I need to get back to see if he's there. I mean, there's no one to let him inside."

"How long's your husband away for?"

"I'm not sure. He's gone on business. It depends how long it takes him to secure the deal."

"What does he do?"

"He works for a small company that makes nutritional supplements for cattle and sheep. He's in sales." Savannah chewed her lip, a little unnerved at all the questions. At least this was one she able to answer truthfully. Daniel was a good salesman, even though he had been finding things hard lately. For some reason, he hadn't been able to sell half as much as he usually did, which was making him angrier and more frustrated than ever. Savannah would like to think this was the only reason she was finding it so hard to live with him, but she knew that wasn't the case. She and Daniel should never have gotten married.

"That's good." Mrs. Hodges seemed satisfied with her story, though it didn't make her feel any easier.

"I think maybe I should try walking a little more with this foot," Savannah said, rubbing the chocolatey crumbs from her fingers. "This cake's lovely, by the way."

"The doctor said you're to rest for a few days," Mrs. Hodges reminded her, stopping her in her tracks as she leaned forward to get up. "If you'll only be going back to an empty house, I think it's best you stay here for a while until it heals. I'm sure the dog will be all right. Maybe Tom and Greg could have a look for him when they finish work."

"Oh, I couldn't ask them to do that." Savannah panicked. It would be easy enough to just let the guys go looking for a non-existent dog — after all, they would only report back later that they couldn't find him — but the sky was dull and it looked as though it was going to rain again. Her conscience wouldn't let her send them on a fool's errand in this weather. "Though, you're right. Willow's probably found his way back home by now and is curled up in the shed we always leave open for him. I'm sure he'll be all right. I'll be back on my feet tomorrow. I can catch up with him then."

"Good, though there's no rush. You stay here as long as you like." Although Mrs. Hodges sounded satisfied, her eyes were a little narrowed, making Savannah wonder if she believed her story.

* * * *

Greg slammed the door of the truck and climbed in beside Tom, who already had the engine revving.

They'd hardly spoken two words to each other all afternoon and the atmosphere was suffocating. To make matters worse, rain started to splatter the windshield as they drove along the track toward town, with mud squelching beneath their tires.

"Okay, I get it. It was my idea to see her," Greg relented, putting his hands up in submission as they neared Mrs. Hodges' house.

He sighed when Tom didn't reply.

"Well, how in hell was I to know what she wanted?" Greg went on.

"It wasn't that hard to guess," Tom grumbled. "Anyone with half an eye could see what she was up to."

"At least she apologized for the way she treated us."

Tom snorted. "Only because she thought she could get us back again. I can't believe the nerve of that girl. She dumps us for that guy, finds he's not as much fun as she thought he'd be and thinks we'll just take her back." He shook his head.

"Gives you a good feeling, though, eh? Knowing she regrets dumping us and wants to come back." Greg snickered.

Tom glanced over at him, his eyebrows raised. "What doesn't feel good is knowing that she thought she'd just get away with it. Do we have 'loser' written across our foreheads or somethin'?"

Greg pouted as the truck came to a halt outside the house. "Well, she knows how we feel now. I think we made ourselves perfectly clear."

"I thought you were a little brutal, to be honest." Tom climbed out of the truck and joined Greg, walking up the tiny path to the front door. "I thought you liked her?"

Greg shook his head. "No one likes to get shit on, buddy. She had no right thinking she could get us back and I wanted her to know that, fair and square. Besides, you didn't say much, so one of us had to speak."

Mrs. Hodges met them at the door. "Supper's almost ready," she told them. "Get washed up and it'll be on the table in twenty minutes."

"Thanks, Mrs. H. You're the best." Greg grinned at her, removing his hat.

"Is Savannah still here?" Tom wanted to know.

Greg rolled his eyes. He knew Tom was sore at him because he'd insisted on meeting up with Frankie when his friend had wanted to come back and see their new houseguest. The fact that Frankie had totally wasted their time had just made matters worse. He couldn't blame Tom for being mad. He was pretty annoyed himself.

"Yeah, she's here," Mrs. Hodges said, closing the door behind them.

Greg was surprised at how relieved he was and noticed Tom's shoulders relax a little, too.

"We'll be right back down," Tom promised, heading for the stairs.

It didn't take long for the guys to get showered and changed.

"You look tired," Savannah said, as they all sat at the table in the little kitchen.

"Yeah, it's been a long day," Greg replied with a smile. She sure was a lovely girl, and it was nice of her to look so concerned when her huge green eyes gazed up at him. Her beauty blew him away. Her long red hair hung in swathes around her shoulders, and her gorgeous face looked just like one of those porcelain dolls his mom used to keep in her glass cabinet.

He was relieved she was okay after her ordeal the previous night and knew Tom would be, too. Almost running her over was just too close to home, and he knew his friend felt dreadful about it. He was a little perturbed to see her up and dressed, though. She still looked quite pale and fragile, making him wonder if she should have stayed in bed. He remembered what a headstrong woman she was, though, so thought it best to say nothing.

Mrs. Hodges served up a delicious beef stew and they all tucked in.

"Those new cattle arrived, then?" Mrs. Hodges asked.

Tom grunted, causing the women to look over at him in surprise.

"Well, they've arrived," Greg explained, "though they're not in quite the good shape any of us were expecting."

"That's some understatement," Tom said, shaking his head. "Matt said that when he saw them, they all looked real healthy, but now they look like they haven't been fed for a week."

"Oh no, that's awful." Savannah frowned, putting her hand to her mouth.

"So, what's he gonna do?" Mrs. Hodges asked, breaking off some of her bread roll.

"Not much he *can* do," Greg replied. "He's contacted the seller, who reckons there's nothing wrong with them. If he wants to send them back, he has to pay the transportation costs, which means he may as well keep them and see what he can salvage. We've got plenty of good pasture for them, and there's half a field of turnips they can have, so they should be okay. It's just the principle of the thing. His brother's looking into ways of getting some kind of compensation for him."

"What's the guy's excuse?" Mrs. Hodges wondered.

"He's shutting down. Obviously thought that once the sale had been agreed, he didn't have to take responsibility for them anymore."

"But it must have been in the agreement?" Savannah pointed out.

"Yeah, it would have been. But the guy's gone bust. If he's declared bankruptcy, there's no point in trying to sue him for breach of contract. You can't get blood from a stone, no matter how hard you squeeze it."

"So, that's why he wasn't able to feed them properly? He had no money." Savannah looked sad.

"Which is exactly why he was selling them in the first place."

She nodded.

"Don't worry. We'll get them fixed up," Greg assured her, noticing how upset she looked about the whole thing.

"Yeah. Maybe your husband could help out with those supplements?" Mrs. Hodges suggested, perking up a little. She turned to the guys. "Savannah's husband's a salesman for a company that makes feed supplements for animals. He might be able to give Matt a good deal."

"That would be great. Matt was going to take a look into something like that after the veterinarian finished with them this morning. He said it's not a thing he normally bothers with — the ground's so good around here that they're not usually needed — but in this case, it might help. The veterinarian was all for it." Tom piped up, suddenly taking an interest.

Savannah's pretty face turned red as all eyes were suddenly on her. "I-I don't know," she murmured.

Greg frowned, sensing a problem. "When's he due home?"

"I'm...er...not sure. He's away on business. It all depends how he gets on. I never know exactly how long he'll be away." She fiddled with her napkin.

"Oh, right." He detected there was no way she'd want her husband dealing with them, but he was curious as to why.

"Well, it was just a thought," Mrs. Hodges said, clearly noticing the uneasiness about the situation. She was quite perceptive.

For a second, Greg thought Savannah was about to burst into tears but realized she was just gearing up for a huge sneeze.

"Hmm, looks like the doc was right about you catching a cold," Mrs. Hodges said, standing to clear away the dishes.

"Sorry." Savannah had gone even redder now with embarrassment. She blew her nose and tucked her handkerchief up her sleeve.

"Looks like you'll be laid up for another day or two," Tom said, smiling at her.

Poor Savannah looked astonished at the idea.

"Oh no, I can't stay. I need to get home."

"Oh, that's right. You need to check on that dog of yours, don't you?" Mrs. Hodges narrowed her eyes a little at Savannah and Greg's mind whirled. The ladies had clearly been talking.

"You have a dog?" he asked in surprise.

Savannah nodded.

"That's why she was out last night, looking for her lost dog." Mrs. Hodges couldn't have made it plainer that she didn't believe a word of it, and Savannah looked horrified.

"What sort of dog?" Tom asked, leaning forward.

Mrs. Hodges cleared the condiments from the table but didn't say anything.

Savannah was almost the color of a beetroot. "He's a mongrel," she said, "brown with white patches on his legs. We got him from a shelter, so I don't know what breeds he is. We were out for a walk when he ran off."

Tom nodded. "Ah, that explains why you were out in the storm last night. We wondered."

Savannah looked even more unnerved, her eyes flitting from Tom to Greg. "He's probably made his way home by now," she said, jutting her chin out a little. "I'm going back tomorrow to make sure he's

42

okay. There's no one there to let him in, you see? He's got a bed made up in the shed, but he'll be hungry."

"Dogs are quite capable animals. He'll have scrounged some food from somewhere," Greg said, trying to make her feel a little easier.

"She lives over at Upton Crossing," Mrs. Hodges said, returning to the table with a tray of coffee. "Shall we take these through?"

"Here. Let me," Tom offered, rising to his feet and taking the tray from her.

"We could run you back if you like?" Greg suggested. "Make sure that dog of yours is okay and get you settled in properly with that ankle."

He had hoped Savannah would look relieved — grateful, even — but she stared at him like a rabbit caught in a truck's headlights. Panic seeped from her every pore as her mouth fell open.

"I— I'm fine," she told him.

He'd put his hand out to help her up and wasn't sure if she meant that she didn't need his help or that she didn't want a ride home. The way her body stiffened made him wonder if she meant both.

"Let's go get that coffee," he coaxed her, trying to sound breezy. "I'm sure I noticed some of Mrs. H's famous chocolate cake in there, too."

"Actually, I'm a little tired. I think I'll just go on up," she said. She stood with the aid of the table, ignoring his hand.

"Let me help you." He caught hold of her arm, which he noticed was trembling.

"I can manage. You go join the others," she insisted.

"I will once I've got you safely up those stairs. They must be hell with that ankle." He was determined not to let her disappear and kept a tight grip on her arm.

"No, really. It's fine now. I think I just twisted it a little. It's not a problem, honestly." She tried to wrench her arm from his hold, but he wasn't letting up.

"The doc seemed to think it was quite severe," he reminded her, his jaw tensing.

"Well, it's not," she snapped back, before whipping out her handkerchief and sneezing into it.

He had no choice but to relinquish his hold on her arm and just stood watching her as she wiped her nose.

"Excuse me," she said, looking up at him with eyes that seemed to be pleading with him.

"Sounds like it might be the flu," Tom announced, appearing in the doorway.

"Yeah. I'm just going to get off to bed," Savannah said, nodding.

She looked up at Greg, and he realized she had been asking him to move, not excusing herself for sneezing. He had no option but to comply, unless he was going to make a big fuss, which just wasn't his style. Besides, he had to agree that bed was the best place for her. He took a step back.

"You're missing out on chocolate cake," Tom pointed out with a smile.

Savannah turned back to face him. "I had some earlier. It's delicious."

Greg couldn't resist putting a hand out to help her as she brushed past him but noticed the way her whole body bristled at his touch.

"Thanks again for all your help last night," she said, as though dismissing them, and Greg stiffened.

"No problem," Tom replied with a wave of his hand as she disappeared through the door.

But there *was* a problem. A very *big* problem.

Chapter Four

Savannah only just reached her bedroom before the tears gushed down her face. Her ankle throbbed and her throat was raw. Her head pounded and her heart ached. It was all too much.

Collapsing in a helpless heap on the bed, she buried her face in the soft, lavender-scented pillow and sobbed as a torrent of pain and misery racked her body and mind. It was as though she were surrounded in nothing but white noise. Everything was loud in her head, as though her own thoughts were shouting at her, but nothing made any sense. There were no words to describe her feelings because she had just stopped thinking and her mind had numbed. Her brain had turned to mush and she could do nothing but let sheer emotion overtake her.

She must have fallen asleep, because she awoke in the dark and the crying had stopped. A miserable calmness engulfed her, almost suffocating her, and she felt weak as a kitten.

Realizing she was still dressed, and her crumpled clothing was clinging to her fevered body, she made her way to the little bathroom down the hall, taking with her the large T-shirt she had worn the night before.

Someone was snoring as she passed one of the bedrooms and she wondered whose room it was. It must have been late, and everyone was in bed, so she dared not wake them with the shower. She stripped off and had a good all-over wash using the facecloth and rose-scented soap Mrs. Hodges had left out for her that morning. After pulling on the T-shirt and cleaning her teeth, she ran a comb though her long hair. She kept it in good condition, so it wasn't as matted as she had feared, and she tied it in a neat plait down one shoulder to keep it tidy.

With a sigh, she gazed at the puffy eyes and red-blotched face that stared back at her in the small mirror. She looked much older than her twenty-four years, and Daniel's comment about her looking like an old woman with her hair tied up came back to haunt her.

She wondered what he was doing now that he was on his own and half-hoped that he regretted treating her so harshly. On the other hand, she knew she was better off without him, no matter how miserable she was right now. Once she was out of here and back on the road, she would feel much better. She looked forward to making a new start, and the farther she was from Daniel when she made it, the better.

A huge sneeze took her by surprise and she grabbed at the toilet tissue then blew her nose. There was no way of doing it quietly and she prayed she hadn't woken anyone. After washing her hands again and grabbing her clothes, she opened the door.

"Are you okay?" Tom stood in just a pair of shorts. His dark gaze looked worried and his smattering of chest hair was enticing.

"Uh…" Savannah's brain turned to mush again, but for a different reason this time. "Um…"

He held a hand out to her.

"Come on. Let's get you back to bed."

He curled his long fingers around the top of her arm as he coaxed her out of the bathroom, then he slung his arm around her shoulder. His whole body was hard and strong against hers, which seemed feeble and small. He smelled faintly of aftershave, but mainly of man.

Savannah was dazed as she allowed him to return her to her room, her ankle still throbbing. It seemed darker than ever after she'd been in the light of the bathroom, but Tom seemed to have no difficulty locating the bed and helping her to get inside.

"Thank you," she whispered, hoping it was dark enough for him not to see how many tissues she had left strewn across the covers from all her crying earlier.

He leaned over her and placed a cool hand on her forehead.

"You're burning up," he murmured. "Looks like it might be the flu, after all. Hang on. I'll fetch you some water."

"No, it's…"

But he was already on his way out of the door, carrying the small jug that Mrs. Hodges had left on her nightstand this morning. Normally, she was sure she'd be feeling nervous having a man in her bedroom, but right now, she felt too poorly to care. She was grateful for the soft pillow beneath her pounding head, and that she had a bed to lie in as her whole body ached like the devil.

"You need to keep your fluids up," he announced in a soft voice when he returned. He poured her a glass of water. "I'll leave that in case you want it later."

"Thank you."

The bed dipped as he sat on it, much to Savannah's surprise. He reached over and straightened the coverlet before stroking her hair.

No one had ever touched her as tenderly as he did when he brushed her cheek, while sweeping a stray curl away from her face.

"You need to get some sleep," he whispered.

She nodded, feeling a weird burn in the pit of her stomach.

"Close your eyes," he urged.

She did as he said, expecting to feel the bed move again as he got up to go. It didn't. She was sure he'd leave any second, but her eyes were too heavy to open. She knew he was still there, because he continued to stroke her hair, and she sighed with contentment. It was a nice feeling. He seemed very calm and in control, but not condescending and bullish like she was used to. She started to relax for the first time in a long time and allowed herself to just lie there, savoring the feeling while she could.

Tom watched as Savannah's features softened and her breathing became a little heavier, indicating that she had gone back to sleep. He loved the feel of her silky hair in his fingers, though he was concerned at how hot her cheek had been when he'd brushed it.

She must have gotten drenched while she was out in that damn storm the other night, and now she was just getting worse. He was glad he had the day off tomorrow so at least he could help look after her.

He grimaced at the idea she was planning to head home in the morning. No way she should make the journey while she was ill, and there would be no one to take care of her when she got there.

He'd sensed a tension between her and Greg in the kitchen tonight and had known she was upset when she'd gone up to bed. At one point, he had thought he'd heard her whimpering when he'd popped upstairs to use the bathroom, but when he'd opened her door, she had been fast asleep, amid a host of crumpled tissues. *Poor thing must have cried herself to sleep.*

She'd looked so frail, much as she did now. He hated that her husband had gone off and left her. He wouldn't even know what had happened. Mrs. H had told them that she had been with Savannah all day and she definitely hadn't used the phone. When they'd spoken about it, it seemed that no one had even seen Savannah with a cell phone, and there hadn't been one in her pocket when Mrs. H had washed her clothes the previous night. She'd checked at the time.

Even though she had only gone out to walk the dog, it seemed odd not to have taken a cell or some money. If she had paid her bus fare, she would surely have had *some* change, let alone a purse or jacket. Her sweater had been stretched out of shape, probably from getting so wet, and she'd only had a thin top on underneath it, hardly the right clothes to wear for a walk outside in winter. And what about her sneakers? They looked worn through. Her feet must have been covered in blisters.

Something didn't ring true in all this, and he was determined to find out what was going on.

Savannah was sleeping peacefully when he rose from her bed and went back to his own.

Greg stirred in the twin bed on the other side of their room, but he didn't speak as Tom slid beneath his covers. He would have liked to have stayed gazing at Savannah all night—she was so pretty—but it just wouldn't be right. It was good to see that she was getting some rest, though. Her tear-stained face had wrenched at his heart when he'd seen her in the bathroom doorway, but his concern was exacerbated by the way her shoulders had slumped, as though she were finding it hard to keep upright.

He cursed himself for not coming back to see her at lunchtime today. Greg had known he'd wanted to spend some time getting to know Savannah instead of succumbing to Frankie's demands. And what a waste of time that had been. So, Jonathan Morgan hadn't been as much fun as she'd thought he'd be. More like, he wouldn't lavish expensive gifts on her like she'd hoped. Mrs. H had told them that guy was very frugal with his money—although Frankie just thought he was mean and stingy.

There was no way he was prepared to give her another chance, as she'd asked—more like pleaded. Greg was more easy-going than him, and Tom had worried at first that he might have been contemplating going ahead with her suggestion, but there was no way Tom was going to agree to it. He'd been surprised when Greg had spoken up, though, and realized that they were both singing from the same hymn-sheet. That girl had made fools of both of them and no one got a second chance at that.

* * * *

Tom knew the minute Savannah awoke the next morning, because she had a coughing fit. He ran upstairs and opened her door to see her sitting up in bed, clutching the glass of water he had poured the previous night. Her hands were trembling so much it looked as though she was about to spill the drink everywhere.

"Here… Let me," he offered, crossing the room in one stride to grab the water from her. He held her back while helping her to take small sips, conscious of the way her whole body seemed to be burning hot.

"She's getting worse," Mrs. Hodges said, coming into the room. "I'll give the doc another ring."

Savannah looked as though she wanted to object, but Tom kept the glass close to her lips so she couldn't speak. Besides, it was more important to get the fluids into her than have an argument — because they would have one. There was no way he would condone her being this ill and not seeing the doctor.

After a pause for another cough, Savannah took one more drink then Tom replaced the glass on the nightstand.

"You'd better stay in bed today," he said, as she moved.

"I need to use the bathroom," she explained, her voice croaky and weak.

Tom nodded. He couldn't argue with that. "Okay."

He pulled back the covers, noticing how damp they were, as she must have sweat all night, and he watched as she slowly swung her legs around to the side of the bed. He'd been right about those blisters. Her feet were covered in them. Some looked like they'd been bleeding.

She winced as she placed her bare feet on the rug, and he wasn't sure if it was the blisters or her sprained ankle that hurt the most. The swelling around her bandage indicated that she might have spent too much time on her feet the day before, despite her protestations that she had been fine. The doc wouldn't be pleased, and neither was he.

"I'll carry you."

Before she could object, he lifted her into his arms and started walking toward the door. To his surprise, she didn't say anything. She tucked her head into his chest and put her arms around his neck. It felt good.

Her whole body burned as though it was on fire as he took her down the corridor.

"She all right?" Greg was just coming out of their room, frowning.

Tom shook his head, not wanting to disturb her, as she seemed so settled.

Greg pouted.

Tom took her into the bathroom.

"You still need to go?" His voice was soft, and he couldn't be sure she hadn't gone back to sleep.

She nodded.

Gently, he lowered her onto the toilet.

"Don't look," she murmured, only just opening her eyes.

"All right. But I'm not leaving you on your own. You'll only fall off."

"What?" Her brow furrowed in confusion.

"Hold onto the seat with that hand and hold mine with the other," he told her, settling her in place. He turned his back, still holding her hot little hand.

Had she been a little more compos mentis, he was sure she would have yelled at him to leave the room, but she seemed barely conscious right now.

"I need the other hand," she murmured, tugging at it, once she'd finished.

"You steady?"

"Yeah."

Reluctantly he let go and heard her roll the tissue. He was desperate to turn around and make sure she was okay but feared upsetting her. The washbasin was right next to the toilet, so he stood facing that instead.

"Stay there. You can wash your teeth while you're sitting down." He rinsed the toothbrush Mrs. Hodges had given her, squirted some paste on it and handed it to her.

If she blushed, he couldn't notice as her face was already red with the fever.

She brushed her teeth then he helped her stand to rinse her mouth, before she washed her face with a cool facecloth.

"Better?"

She nodded.

While she washed her hands, he flushed the toilet before washing his own.

Another coughing fit ensued before he was able to scoop her back into his arms and return her to her room.

Mrs. Hodges was at the top of the stairs when they came down the corridor and her eyebrows nearly disappeared behind her hair rollers when she saw them come out of the bathroom together.

"The doc's on his way," she said, as Tom put Savannah back into her bed.

He pulled the cover over her, her eyes fluttering as she drifted back to sleep.

"Good," he replied. "I'll stay with her until he arrives."

Chapter Five

Savannah drifted in and out of sleep all day, vaguely conscious of Mrs. Hodges coming and going. Tom was there almost every time she awoke, but she didn't feel up to talking, which seemed to suit him just fine.

It was supper time before she had the strength to sit up in bed and drink the soup Tom fed her by the spoonful.

"How are you feeling now?" he asked, his voice smooth as velvet.

Her headache wasn't as bad as it had been, and her throat was soothed by the warm soup. She still ached all over, though.

"Fine." She nodded.

"And how do you *really* feel?"

She sighed, realizing he wasn't about to take her word for it.

"Not as bad as before," she relented. "I still ache everywhere." Her voice was croaky and it took effort to get the words out.

He seemed satisfied with that answer.

"So, why did you say you were fine?"

He wasn't letting it go.

She shrugged, not wanting to tell him the truth—that she was used to saying she was 'fine' because it made no difference to Daniel, even if she felt like she was dying. He'd only tell her to get over it, and she'd be expected to carry on as normal with the housework and cooking his meals.

He pursed his lips, indicating that he wasn't happy with her response, but he wasn't pushing it any further.

When she'd finished the soup, he offered her the last of the bread and placed the bowl back onto the tray.

The bread was fresh and soft, and she couldn't stop a moan of appreciation escaping her.

Tom raised an eyebrow as he looked back at her, making her blush as she realized what she'd done.

"Have you had enough?"

She nodded.

"Mrs. H is keen to change your bedding before you go to sleep tonight, so do you feel up to sitting in this chair?"

Savannah felt like she'd just been offered the crown jewels. She'd been in bed all day and relished the idea of getting away from the sweaty covers.

"Could I take a shower?"

Tom chuckled. He looked even more handsome when he smiled. "Whoa. Hold your horses. Maybe tomorrow." He must have noticed her face fall because he added, "but I might be able to rustle up a clean T-shirt for you, if it'll make you feel any better?"

Something lurched inside her. "Yes, please." She looked down at the one she was wearing. "Is this yours, then?"

"The Mavericks?" He gave a horrified look, indicating the faded band picture on the front of it. "You've got to be kidding! No, it's most definitely one of Greg's. I'll get you a decent one for tonight. You must have had nightmares in that thing."

Despite feeling so rotten, she snickered.

"All done?" Mrs. Hodges came in to retrieve the tray.

"It was lovely. Thank you," Savannah told her with a nod.

"Well, I must say, you're looking a little better now. Good to see you smiling, too."

"I feel better," Savannah told her.

"You've been on some pretty strong meds," she replied. "Hopefully you'll feel more like yourself tomorrow. The doc'll be here to check on you again in the morning."

"She's looking forward to getting out of bed," Tom said. "I'll lift her onto this chair while we put on some fresh sheets."

"You do that. I'll be back with some bedding in a minute."

After Mrs. Hodges left the room, Savannah leaned forward to Tom. "I could use the bathroom again, if you don't mind?" She was a little embarrassed. She knew he'd taken her this morning but couldn't quite remember how it had worked. She must have been really out of it then.

"No problem." His smile was kind and understanding.

She was relieved as he pulled the covers off her heated body. Then she shivered at the change in temperature.

"Cold?"

"Not really." She shook her head, glad that her hair was tied up. "It was just the contrast, I think."

"We'd better make it quick, then. Don't want you getting any worse. Do you want a blanket?"

"No, thanks."

Not only would it make her hot again, she knew it would be a hindrance once she reached the bathroom.

She placed her clammy arms around his neck and he lifted her out of the bed. He smelled lovely. Fresh. She breathed him in while listening to his steady, strong heartbeat as he carried her down the corridor.

Savannah was quite embarrassed when he set her on the toilet.

"You'll have to wait outside," she told him.

Tom bit his lip.

"Are you sure you'll be all right?" He narrowed his eyes.

"Yes, of course, I..." Her stomach dropped as a recollection of earlier flashed in her mind. Tom had stayed with her this morning. She remembered him being there, standing in front of her while she...

"Something wrong?" He was frowning now.

"You need to wait outside," she reiterated. "I can manage the next part."

He gave a satisfied nod.

"I'll be right outside the door," he promised.

She rolled her eyes.

"You just holler if you need anything – or if you start feeling woozy or whatever."

"I will."

Finally, he left her alone.

She gripped the sides of the seat for dear life, realizing that she wasn't quite as 'fine' as she had insisted. Her head swam a little and she began to shiver.

She pulled the flush then took the couple of steps to the sink. Her ankle throbbed and she winced as she put her weight on it.

The cold water was a blessing, and she washed her face with one hand while clinging to the washbasin like a limpet with the other. She peered into the mirror and was surprised at how flushed she looked. Then her image became blurry and her body seemed weaker than ever.

"Ugh!" she moaned. It was all she could manage.

The next moment, strong arms caught her as she was about to fall.

"Whoa!" Tom whisked her back up into his arms again.

"I...I'm sorry. I just felt—"

"Like you were about to pass out?"

"Not exactly. Just—"

"Never mind. Let's get you back to your room. You're shivering."

With her arms wrapped around his neck, she closed her eyes as colors merged around her. The dizziness eased as she relaxed into his taut chest, and his steady heartbeat soothed her.

"I've changed the bed," Mrs. Hodges announced as soon as they reached the bedroom.

"I'll put her straight into it," Tom said.

Savannah was a little disappointed that she couldn't sit in the chair for a change, but she really did feel quite weak, so surmised that bed was the best place for her right now.

"Is she still with us?" Mrs. Hodges asked, as Tom straightened the covers.

"Yeah."

"Must be the drugs. Doc said they were strong. Still, they must be doing some good."

Savannah could hear them talking about her but didn't have the strength to open her eyes, let alone respond.

"Get some sleep, beautiful," Tom murmured, then kissed her very on the forehead.

Her insides went hot for a second. *He just kissed me.* Tom was a very handsome cowboy, and she felt safe in his arms, but she hadn't expected a kiss — or to be called beautiful. She was a married woman, for goodness' sake.

Her mind whirled. Sure, she was married, but what did all that mean now? Now that he'd slung her out? Daniel didn't want her, and she certainly didn't want him. She knew he'd only married her because she had been pregnant. When she'd miscarried, he'd felt cheated — not in the way that she had, deprived of the little life that had started growing inside her. Daniel's concern was that they '*didn't need to get married after all*' and that had he known what was going to happen, he would have thought twice. But no one could have known. The doctor had said it was just '*one of those things*'.

Savannah had come to terms with losing her baby, but she'd had a hard time accepting that she was now married to someone who despised her. He'd even accused her of luring him into marriage, of using him. Although it was more likely that his father had insisted he 'do the right thing' and marry her.

He had often said they should never have married and he was right. It didn't make sense that he was so averse to the idea of a divorce, though. And to throw her out of the house with nothing was just —

"Shh."

She heard Tom soothe her and realized she must have whimpered. Hearing him reminded her where she was and who she was with. She'd been in such a hurry to get on her way the day before, but now she could see that she was lucky to be there, to be looked after by such kind people.

She sighed at the thought before drifting into a peaceful sleep.

Tom sat watching Savannah. She seemed more peaceful now than she had earlier. He'd seen her eyelids flutter and she frowned, like she was thinking about something awful. Tears had pooled around her long lashes, she'd let out a little cry and he couldn't help wondering what was upsetting her. He had managed to soothe her into a more relaxed sleep, and she had now slumbered for a couple of hours while he held her hand over the coverlet.

He was glad. She needed her rest. Her breathing wasn't as labored as before, and she seemed to be less clammy.

"How is she?"

He looked around to see that Greg had returned home. "Better than she was."

Greg nodded, holding onto the doorframe. "Mrs. H said you've been with her all day."

"Yup." Tom looked back at Savannah.

"I'll just get showered then I'll take over, if you like. Give you a break."

"No need." Tom was still gazing at her.

Greg snorted before disappearing to get cleaned up.

Tom didn't even look up as he heard Greg enter the room a short while later. He could smell the fresh aftershave and guessed he was feeling better for having gotten washed and changed.

He knew what was coming next and it was the last thing he needed.

"Hope you're not getting too attached."

And there it was.

"I think she's in some kind of trouble," Tom replied, still watching Savannah sleep.

"I kind of guessed that much. Has she said anything?"

"Nope. Not really."

"I spoke to the sheriff earlier. There's been no reports of a stray dog around the area."

Tom nodded.

"So, she was out in the middle of the night in a thunderstorm, with no purse or coat in the middle of winter because…?"

Looking up at him, Tom sighed. "Beats me."

"Sheriff's asking around to see if he can come up with anything."

Tom stared at him, his body burning. "What?"

Greg shrugged, looking back over at Savannah. He was standing next to the bed now, looking refreshed. "I had to do something."

"So, you blurted out her business to the sheriff? What the hell possessed you to do that?" Tom's voice rose at the same time he did, standing and squaring up to his buddy.

Greg sighed. "Look. We don't know who she is or why she was out there, but we *do* know something ain't right. I just thought Dyson might be able to find out where she's missing from. What's wrong with that?"

"And what if she's running from someone? What if she's in danger? What if Dyson is about to tell the very person she's trying to escape from exactly where she is?"

Greg shook his head. "She's with us. If she's hiding for whatever reason, we can protect her. Dyson won't let anyone near her if she doesn't want to see them. I just think we owe it to her to try to help."

"We *owe* it to her to respect her privacy. If she wanted to be found, don't you think she'd have gone to the sheriff herself?" Tom clenched his fists as he spoke through gritted teeth.

"In case it has escaped your notice, she's not exactly in a fit state to go around looking for the sheriff." Greg rolled his eyes.

"You had no right!"

"What's all this noise?" Mrs. Hodges scurried in, frowning.

"Ask him," Tom said, sulking.

"Me? You're the one hollering in the room with a poorly woman who's trying to sleep!" Greg protested, his voice rising.

"Why don't you guys go downstairs and talk?" Mrs. Hodges suggested. "I'll stay with Savannah for a while."

Tom's gut twisted. He didn't want to leave her, but he was also desperate to hear Greg's explanation for doing such a heinous thing. He said nothing but left the room and made his way down to the living room, closely followed by Greg.

"You could have just put that poor girl in danger. Do you realize that?" Tom spat out, not even bothering to sit down.

"Has she said anything about being in danger?" Greg took a seat, his voice too calm for Tom's liking.

"No. Like I said, she hasn't said anything. As you so kindly pointed out, she's not exactly one hundred percent at the moment, is she? I was hoping she might confide in us when she was feeling a little better, and when she had learned she could trust us. Seems that ship has sailed, thanks to you!" Tom pointed at him.

"What if something's happened to her and she can't remember anything? It's hardly normal behavior to be out in a thunderstorm in the middle of nowhere, let alone at night. She might have had an accident. Someone else could be involved. What if she's got people out there looking for her right now, worried sick that she's just disappeared? How would you feel if that were you?" Greg seemed to have it all thought out.

Tom shook his head. "You still shouldn't have done anything without asking her first. We don't know anything about her." His words were clipped.

"We know she's married. Has she actually contacted her husband since she's been here?" Greg pointed out.

"She's not well and her husband's away. Why worry him needlessly?"

"And you believe all that, do you?"

Tom frowned, a little taken aback. "She's wearing a wedding ring."

"That doesn't prove anything."

"It proves you've got a suspicious mind. She's done nothing to suggest she's been lying to us. Why would you doubt her?"

Greg sighed, running his hand through his fair hair that fell forward a little onto his face. "I'm not saying I don't trust her."

"But?"

"But she might be confused. She's had a fever. Maybe she's not thinking straight. I just want to help her out, find out what's going on."

"So, *ask* her, dipshit!" Tom growled out the words.

"I will. I just thought it might help if the sheriff was able to keep his ear to the ground." He put his hands up in a placating manner, which did nothing to ease Tom's fury.

"If you've put her life in danger with your big mouth, I'll—"

"You'll what?" Greg was on his feet now.

Tom bit his lip, trying to curb his wrath. Greg was his best friend and he didn't want to fight with him, but he couldn't help feeling loyal to the helpless woman he had just spent the day caring for.

"You should've checked first." Tom stormed out of the room and slammed the front door behind him when the cold evening air took his breath away.

Chapter Six

Savannah awoke a couple of times during the night. It was dark, save for the moonlight peering through a gap in the drapes, and she was alone. She felt peaceful, safe. She'd escaped Daniel. Okay, so she'd had no choice in the matter, but it was probably for the best. She had worried that his aversion to divorce might cause him to try to keep her against her will. At least she had her freedom now, despite having nothing else.

Her mind whirled with possibilities. She might be far enough away by now to start a new life. It was a nice thought, and one that carried her back into peaceful slumber.

Eventually she woke to find sunlight trying to force its way through the thick fabric of the curtains. She was content and even her headache had eased.

"You've had a good sleep." Mrs. Hodges arrived with a breakfast tray. "You must be starving by now, too."

A quick inventory of her body told Savannah that she was hungry. She nodded, pulling herself into a sitting position while the older lady repositioned her pillows.

"I feel much better," Savannah told her, taking the cup of coffee she was offered.

"Good. The doc gave you some strong medication yesterday — probably why you slept so long. He'll be by to see you shortly. In the meantime, eat your oatmeal."

Savannah wasted no time in complying. It was delicious.

"How far away are we from Upton Crossing?" she asked, her mouth half full.

Mrs. Hodges sat down. "Well, now... It's eight miles to Almondine from here, and I'd say Upton's about another ten or more miles from there. Upton Crossing's even farther on than that, isn't it? You've come a fair way."

Savannah went warm inside. That meant she was safe.

"You're not planning to go back just yet, are you?" the old lady asked. "We'd have to check with the doc, but I'd be surprised if..."

"No. I'm in no hurry," Savannah replied with a smile. "Thank you for looking after me."

"Oh, think nothing of it. It's just how we roll around here, helping one another out." Mrs. Hodges stood and took the tray from the nightstand. "D'you need anything?"

"Are...are the guys working today?" Savannah tried not to sound too interested.

"Sure are. I think they're having some trouble with those poor half-starved cattle Matt Shearer bought. Dreadful business, if you ask me." She shook her head as she left the room.

Savannah leaned back against the soft pillows. The scent of lavender wafted around the room, while the sunlight continued to strain against the drapes, barely squeezing through the gap to leave a bright stream onto the floor.

Pelican's Heath seemed like a nice place to be, if Mrs. Hodges and the guys were anything to go by. She loved that these people were willing to take in a perfect stranger and care for her without too many questions. She might consider settling here. There were a few things to sort out first, though, like how she was going to live with no money, no home and no clothes.

She must have dozed off as she awoke to hear Mrs. Hodges coming back into the room with a tray of coffee and cake.

"I didn't mean to disturb you," she said, frowning.

"You're not." Savannah scooted back up to a full sitting position, smelling the lemon cake as soon as Mrs. Hodges put the tray down.

"That's good. You've got a visitor."

Savannah smiled, expecting to see the gray-haired doctor that had come before. Instead, it was a handsome man with short, dark hair and a kind smile that entered. Staring up at him, Savannah couldn't help noticing the silver star that glistened from his chest.

"This is Dyson Shearer, the sheriff," Mrs. Hodges told her with a wave of her hand.

"Good morning." He placed his hat on the side of the bed and sat down, as Mrs. Hodges had gestured. "I hope you're feeling better. I hear you've been quite poorly."

Savannah's throat was tight and her mouth was suddenly as dry as a bone. She nodded, trying to control the way her whole body was now trembling.

"Here you go, sheriff." Mrs. Hodges handed him a cup of coffee.

"Thank you, ma'am."

Savannah's cup rattled in its saucer when Mrs. Hodges passed it over and she gave a little nervous laugh.

"Looks like you're still a little feverish," Mrs. Hodges remarked with a frown.

"I'm — I'm fine, really."

"Well, now. I believe your name is Savannah Edgerton. Is that right?" The sheriff consulted his notebook.

"Yes."

"And you've come all the way from Upton Crossing looking for your dog?"

"Yes."

"I've got a description here. Brown and white mongrel. I'm afraid no one's reported seeing him around these parts." The sheriff took a swig of his coffee, and Savannah was unsure whether she was supposed to reply to that or not. She just nodded, wishing he would stand and leave.

He didn't.

"I hear you've been here a couple of days, now," he went on, glancing at her.

"That's right, sheriff. Tom and Greg found her out in the storm the other night. In a right state she was." Mrs. Hodges' interjection reminded Savannah that the lady hadn't even left the room, as she'd expected — or rather, hoped.

"And you've a husband back at home. What's his name?" The sheriff took up his pen, ready to jot down the details.

"Sheriff, have I done something wrong?" Savannah asked.

He stared at her. "Of course not. Or, at least, I don't *think* so. Why do you ask?"

"Then why are you here? Why are you asking me all these questions?" Savannah fought to keep the quiver from her voice and she flushed.

She noticed the sheriff and Mrs. Hodges exchange a look, and a lump hit the pit of her stomach. They suspected something. It was hardly surprising, really. She had just questioned the sheriff, who was only verifying who she was. She must have guilt written all over her face. She swallowed hard, suddenly unable to face the delicious-looking cake in front of her.

"It just seems like you might need some help," the sheriff replied, putting down his pen. "I mean, being out in the middle of the night in a thunderstorm without so much as a purse with you, seems a little…unusual. Don't you think?"

"No. I was looking for my dog. What would you expect me to do? Just leave him because it starts raining?"

"Some people might," he replied. "Why didn't you?"

Savannah bit her lip. "Because he's my dog. I'm responsible for him. I took him out and I wanted to take him home again. Is that a crime?" she spat the words out, anger boiling inside her. *Why is he here? What does he want? What does he know?*

"No. But you must have noticed it was getting late. And you were a long way from home. Why didn't you just go back? Retrace your steps? What made you think the dog would come all the way out here?"

She swallowed hard, trying to think of a logical answer. There wasn't one. It didn't make sense. Surely any normal person who lost a dog would backtrack to try to find him, not keep walking. *Damn!*

"I-I thought I saw him...ahead of me on the way out of Almondine. That's why I came this way."

"I see." The sheriff took up his pen again and jotted something in his notebook before taking a bite of Mrs. Hodges' lemon cake. "This is delicious," he said, smiling at the lady.

Savannah was irritated and unnerved.

"Has someone sent you here?" she asked, narrowing her eyes at him.

He raised his eyebrows in surprise. "Like who?"

She shrugged. "I don't know. I just... How did you know I was here?" Her heart pounded as she awaited his reply.

"Greg Jackson mentioned it to me while he was at the ranch yesterday. Said they'd found you on the back road the other night and asked about your dog. I promised to make inquiries. Turns out no one's seen him." He frowned. "Is that a problem?"

Savannah's breath hitched. *Greg? He went to the sheriff about me? I thought he was a friend!*

"They were going to go searching for the dog," Mrs. Hodges added.

Savannah took a deep breath. Despite betraying her, it was just possible Greg had been trying to help. If he and Tom were prepared to look for her dog, it kind of made sense that they might inquire of the sheriff whether anyone had reported seeing him. It didn't make it any easier to accept, though.

"N-No, of course not," she lied and tried to let out a little laugh.

It was clear no one was buying it.

"Is there anyone you'd like me to contact for you? Your husband, perhaps?" The sheriff was studying her closely now, which freaked the hell out of her.

"Oh, no. Thank you. He's away, so I don't want to worry him. Besides, there's nothing to tell him, really. He'll be assuming I'm at home safe. I'm just here safe, instead." She shrugged, though she knew it didn't look as natural and blasé and she hoped.

The sheriff nodded. "Well, in that case, I'll leave you in peace. Be sure to call me if you need anything, Mrs. Edgerton."

Savannah forced a smile, inwardly cursing herself for giving her real name. Savannah Edgerton from Upton Crossing. How hard would it be to look her up and see that her husband was there, at home? *Why am I so damned stupid?*

She thumped the bed as soon as the sheriff and Mrs. Hodges had left the room. She'd felt so safe and happy here just a short while ago, but now she knew she had to leave…fast.

Quickly getting out of bed, she tested her foot on the floor. It was painful but bearable to walk. She went straight to the bathroom and had a good wash and cleaned her teeth. She combed her hair and tied it up into a neat ponytail, then returned to the bedroom to find her clothes.

"Is everything all right?" Mrs. Hodges returned just as Savannah was forcing her battered sneaker over her swollen foot.

"Yes, of course." She tried hard to look natural. "It's just… Well…the sheriff talking about my dog. It's reminded me that he must be out there somewhere. I need to find him." She forced another smile.

"I thought we'd surmised that he'd probably found his way home and would be curled up in that nice warm bed you've made for him in the shed?" Mrs. Hodges frowned.

"Let's hope so. I'll soon find out."

"You're going now? To Upton Crossing?"

"Yes."

"How?"

"What?"

"How will you get there? You've no money. You can't walk all that way, even if you hadn't sprained your ankle."

The air escaped from Savannah's lungs. She hadn't considered that. Her mouth fell open as her brain searched for answers.

The doorbell sounded, making her jump.

"That'll be the doctor. I don't know what he'll have to say about you being out of bed, let alone planning to go all that way." Mrs. Hodges clearly wasn't pleased as she left the room and went downstairs.

Savannah momentarily considered making a run for it, out of the window and over the yard before they came back upstairs. *But with this ankle?*

"Here she is, doctor."

She gaped at the old man, who frowned back at her.

"What's all this about you going back to Upton Crossing?"

"I live there." Savannah tried to sound matter-of-fact, but the look on his face showed the doctor wasn't happy.

"You won't get far on that ankle. I can see it's swollen from here." He indicated her leg, and she noticed that the swelling did, in fact, show.

"I'll put it up once I get home."

"*If* you get home." He turned back to Mrs. Hodges. "Well, if I'm not needed here, I've got plenty of patients who *do* want my help."

The old lady looked embarrassed as she threw Savannah an unhappy look then led the doctor back downstairs.

Savannah wanted the ground to swallow her whole. It hadn't been her intention to upset the lady who had been so kind to her these past few days.

She didn't want to stay there and answer any more questions, though. With a sigh, she sat back on the bed as a phone rang in the hallway. She heard Mrs. Hodges answer it and waited for her to finish before making her way down the steps. The stairs were steeper than she recalled, and she tried hard not to wince at the pain in her ankle as she slowly went to join the old lady.

"I really am grateful for all your help," she said, trying to smile, when she finally reached the hallway.

"That was Greg ringing to check you were okay. I told him you were just leaving without saying goodbye. The guys are on their way over. Seems Matt Shearer's got some business over at Upton, so they've asked if they can tag along, take you home at the same time. They'll only be a few minutes." Mrs. Hodges sounded a little curt, Savannah noticed.

"Oh…no…really, there's no need."

"They're going that way anyhow. May as well offer a neighbor a ride. I told you. That's how we roll around here."

Savannah sighed much more loudly than she'd intended to. She just couldn't argue with the logic, much as she wanted to. Then again, she could hardly turn up at home with the two guys and their boss in tow. Daniel didn't want her. That was why she was here. But she couldn't explain that to them. How humiliating would it be to admit that her own husband had thrown her out? No, there had to be another way.

"Mrs. Hodges, I really am grateful to you for all you've...ooh." Savannah reached out for the wall of the hallway, one hand on the side of her head.

"Are you all right, dear?" The old lady was next to her in a second, putting a hand on Savannah's shoulder as she slumped against the wall then slid down to the floor.

"Oh, no! Savannah. Savannah, open your eyes, dear."

But Savannah kept her eyes firmly shut.

She heard Mrs. Hodges take the two steps down the hallway to where a phone stood on the table.

"Greg? Come quickly. Savannah's passed out. I can't move her." She sounded panicked. "Oh, thank goodness. Right, then." She replaced the receiver and went straight to the front door.

Savannah shivered as the cold air rushed in and suddenly was glad that she wasn't going out in that weather without a coat.

A few minutes later, Mrs. Hodges was calling out. "I'm so glad you're here. She was about to leave but then she just..."

Heavy footsteps neared her and two strong arms scooped her up and carried her upstairs. Greg, she surmised, by the fresh aftershave. Tom's was muskier, she'd noticed the day before.

She was used to acting in front of Daniel, usually trying to act happy, so it wasn't hard to pretend to be unconscious as she was lowered gently onto the bed.

"Good luck taking those jeans off." Tom's voice.

"Jesus!" Greg must have noticed the swelling of her ankle, and he carefully eased off her jeans while

Savannah gritted her teeth to keep from screaming at the pain.

"What did the doctor say?" Greg asked.

"He didn't examine her. She was already dressed and about to leave when he got here." Mrs. Hodges couldn't hide her disdain.

"We might need to call him back," Tom said.

"He won't be happy," Mrs. Hodges warned them.

There was the sound of someone clearing their throat, probably downstairs.

"We have to go," Greg said, clearly unhappy at the prospect.

"She'll have to stay with us a little longer," Tom said with a sigh. "Poor thing. Looks like she couldn't wait to get home, too."

"Well, we can't take her and just leave her on her own, despite what she says," Greg said.

"I'll look after her. You boys better get off. Don't want you losing your jobs or nothin'," Mrs. Hodges urged.

"Okay." Tom sounded reluctant to leave.

"All right. We shouldn't be late coming back tonight. Call if you need anything, Mrs. H." Greg didn't sound too happy, either, Savannah noticed, before hearing footsteps disappear downstairs and out the door.

She felt Mrs. Hodges lay a thin blanket over her then she, too, left the room.

Chapter Seven

"Is she all right?" Matt Shearer asked as they all climbed back into the truck.

"Yeah. Looks like she just passed out," Tom said. "I think she's not as strong as she'd like to believe."

"Pity. Although I don't want to see her gone, it would be interesting to see where she lives." Greg pursed his lips.

"Well, Upton Crossing's not that big. I'm sure we could ask around while we're over that way, if you want to?" Matt suggested as they drove out of town.

Tom and Greg exchanged a look.

"Nah, it would seem like going behind her back," Greg replied, much to Tom's relief.

"True. I guess I hadn't thought of it like that," Matt said.

"Mrs. H will call the doc back out this afternoon," Tom added. "Once she's back on her feet properly, I'm sure she'll tell us anything we want to know."

Greg gave him a disbelieving look.

After that they fell silent for a while, so Matt put on some country music to fill the void until they neared the town of Upton.

"Is this where the offices are?" Greg asked, looking out of the window at a few shops.

"I'm not sure. We're meeting a guy called Bramhall in a diner here in the main street," Matt said.

"I thought we'd get to see where the stuff's made," Tom remarked, a little disappointed.

"This is how business is often conducted in these parts," Matt said with a grin. "Besides, we're only making inquiries at this stage. I'm sure there'll be time for the grand tour if and when we decide to go ahead with it."

"So, they can't divulge any company secrets," Greg said with a nod. "Shrewd move."

They pulled up in the parking lot just outside a small diner and got out. The cold wind whipped around them, and they were all glad to get inside. It was quite empty except for a few elderly folk and a couple of men sitting in a corner.

"He must be one of those two." Matt led the way, and both men rose as they got closer.

"Matt Shearer?" A portly guy in a white cowboy hat held out his hand.

"Yes, sir."

"I'm Pete Bramhall. This is Dan Edgerton." He indicated a smarmy-looking guy with a false leer across his face, and Matt shook his hand.

"I'd like to introduce Greg Jackson and Tom Rankin." Matt stepped back to let them shake hands, but Tom couldn't stop staring at the second man.

"Good to meet you," Greg said, giving Tom a small shove.

"Yes, how d'ya do?" Tom took a step forward and shook both men's clammy hands.

"Well, shall we get some coffee — or would you prefer something stronger, guys? There's a bar just down the road there." Pete pointed toward the window.

"No, no, coffee's fine. We've got a long drive back," Matt replied with a pleasant smile before sitting down.

The waitress arrived, and Pete ordered the drinks while Tom grabbed a chair from a spare table and they all sat around looking at one another.

"Of course. You've come all the way from Pelican's Heath, haven't you?" Dan said, narrowing his eyes slightly.

"That's right." Matt nodded.

"So, how's business over there? It's an area we haven't looked at yet, but if you think our supplements are needed over that way, it might be worth a trip out." Dan looked quite excited at the prospect.

"Business is great," Matt replied. "Unfortunately, I've just bought myself a herd of cattle that aren't looking so good, so I'm considering your product as a way of boosting their feed a bit. I'm sure it's just a little malnutrition, nothing to worry about."

"Our supplements are a boon to any animal's feed, not just those in need of a little...help," Pete said.

"We don't usually need stuff like that where we are," Greg cut in. "The pasture over our way's grade-A quality. It usually suffices for our livestock. It's just a little unfortunate that a few of our newer cows are a little lean. A mix-up with the seller."

Tom shot him a look, wondering if he meant to sound so curt. He had taken a dislike to the men, especially on hearing that one had the same surname as the woman they had just rescued. It could be coincidence, but a horrid feeling in Tom's gut told him it wasn't.

"So, how big an order are you looking at, first off?" Pete asked Matt, a hungry look in his eyes.

"Well, now, that all depends," he replied with a slight frown, as he sat forward.

"I'll just use the bathroom. Excuse me, gentlemen," Tom said, getting up.

"Let me show you where it is," Dan offered, following him.

Tom was quite capable of following the sign but guessed that the guy would be hoping to get some of the lowdown on the ranch from him. After all, he was only a ranchhand, as far as these people were concerned. In fact, Matt Shearer never made anyone feel like 'only' anything, and he knew he was a valued and trusted member of the staff.

"So, you live in Upton?" Tom asked, as soon as Dan caught up with him.

"Just outside," he replied.

"Seems like a nice area," Tom said, opening the door to the bathroom, allowing Dan to go first.

"It is. Actually, in Upton Crossing, where I live, it's a little more rural — much quieter than out here."

"Upton Crossing? Where the railway is?"

"Yup. Pretty little place."

They took their places at the urinals.

"So, you work for Matt Shearer, then?" Dan inquired. *Duh!* "Yup."

"He's got a good reputation, so I hear."

"Yeah, he's a good guy. Works hard." Tom wondered where all this was leading.

"But I guess the money could be better, huh?" *Ah, so that's where.*

"You hear me complaining?"

"No, but I know a ranch hand doesn't earn all that much. If you ever want to supplement your income a little, why don't you give me a call?"

Tom was only grateful the guy didn't hand him his card then and there.

"You're married?" Tom inquired, once they'd finished.

Dan was washing his hands and looked at his ring, where Tom had gestured. His face fell.

"Yeah. Well...I was."

"Sorry. I didn't mean to pry." Tom dried his hands, his stomach churning.

"Oh, no, it's all right," Dan assured him. "My wife died recently."

"Oh, man, that's awful." Tom watched a vein in Dan's neck twitch.

"Yeah, it was." Dan's eyes darted to Tom's.

"Was it an accident?" Usually, Tom wouldn't dream of being so nosey, but something just didn't seem right about all this. And, besides, they'd never meet again, so what did it matter if some shifty-looking salesman thought he was rude? He'd been called worse things in his time.

Dan sighed. "Yeah."

"Oh, don't tell me — the dang railway? I heard there are some dreadful accidents on that track — something to do with insecure fencing or something. Please tell me it wasn't anything to do with that?" Tom frowned, trying to look concerned.

The tic in Dan's neck went into overdrive. "Yeah, 'fraid so. She was walking down there late one night. I'd told her umpteen times not to take the short-cut, but...well, you know what women are like."

"Oh, yeah, tell me about it." Tom nodded. "They never listen." He hated himself for saying things like that but had to play along if he was going to learn anything.

"That's exactly what Savannah was like. Never listened to a word I said." An angry frown suddenly covered Dan's face.

"Savannah? That's a real pretty name." Tom's jaw tensed, as he wondered just what other lies this guy was telling everyone.

"Yeah. She was a pretty woman," Dan said, as though suddenly remembering he was supposed to be mourning her instead of berating her.

"So, she crossed the track and got hit by a train, I take it?" Tom asked. It felt like he was pulling teeth.

"Yeah, that's about it. Dreadful business."

"I'm real sorry, man." Tom tried his best to sound sincere — *not that this guy would know what sincerity was, even if someone hit him over the head with it!*

"Yeah, well…It's all a bit raw, so I don't talk about it much," Dan said, looking at his feet.

"I can understand that. How long ago was it?

"Just a few weeks."

"I can't imagine what you're going through."

"No one can." Dan pulled open the door, allowing Tom to leave first. "By the way, you might want this. Just call me if you're interested. I reckon you could sell this stuff with your eyes closed." He handed Tom his card. "It's real good commission."

Turning back around to face him, as soon as they'd left the bathroom, Tom couldn't resist asking, "So, any kids or pets to comfort you through all this?"

Dan shook his head. "No."

"That's a shame. I mean... I know it would be more responsibility and all, but there's nothing like...say...a dog or something to keep you company."

"A dog? Don't get me started. I wouldn't give one houseroom. Dirty, stinking animals... I'm better off without that, thanks very much."

Tom forced himself to chuckle. "Sorry, man. It was just a thought."

They returned to find that the waitress had left their drinks, and the guys were deep in conversation.

"Well, if you'd like to recommend us to a few of your locals, I'm sure we could come to some agreement regarding a discount," Pete was saying, his grin widening.

"Actually, I couldn't recommend something I hadn't used myself...and seen good results with," Matt replied with a charming smile.

"All right. What if we offer you a discount on the next batch?" Pete asked, as though it was already a done deal.

Tom was a little concerned that their boss might have made a decision already.

"The *next* batch? You mean one batch won't be strong enough to replace all the nutrients those cattle need? I thought you said this stuff was good?" Greg scowled.

"Oh, it is. But, like we said, you can give this to *all* your animals, not just the malnourished ones." Pete seemed eager to allay their doubts.

"But—like *I* said—our pasture's always been good enough for our livestock without any medical intervention. This is just a one-off occurrence, one unfortunate herd." Greg sounded irritated.

Pete sighed, looking back at Matt, which seemed to annoy Greg even more.

"He's right," Matt said. "I was hoping one batch would do the trick. Just give them a boost."

"Yes…and it will." Dan interjected. "But once you see how effective it is, you'll want it for all your cattle, believe me. This stuff works miracles." He grinned, and Tom couldn't help thinking how quickly he'd switched from grieving widower to tough businessman. *Too damn quickly*.

"Well, I'll take a good look through all these statistics and so forth," Matt said, holding up some papers while pushing back his chair. "And I'll be in touch. I just need to know how much cash we're talking?"

"For one batch?" Pete clarified.

"Yeah."

"It's cheaper if you buy more than one batch at a time," Dan cut in. "Maybe you could split it with one of your neighbors?"

"Provided you don't want to use it for all your livestock then take a discount on the next lot, once your neighboring farmers have seen the results?" Pete added quickly.

"I'll think about it," Matt promised, scraping his chair against the wooden floor as he stood.

Pete and Dan exchanged a panicked expression.

"We were rather hoping you'd make a decision today," Pete admitted.

Matt frowned. "Can you put me in touch with some other farmers who've used this stuff? I'd like to see the results for myself first."

"We'd need to set something up—speak to them beforehand, make sure they're happy to speak to you," Dan said.

"I was rather hoping to just drop in on my way back, if any of them are out this way?" Matt said, narrowing his eyes a little.

"Can't you at least give us the names of local farmers who use it?" Greg asked, clearly suspicious.

"Well…" Dan looked less than unsure.

"Yeah, we could just call them, maybe have a chat about it over the phone," Tom added, enjoying the discomfort of the two businessmen.

"Er… Well…you see, the thing is, it wouldn't be ethical to give out another man's information. Privacy protection and all that. We'd need to get their permission first. Some farmers don't want others knowing their business." Pete stood up.

"So, they don't *all* get a discount for spreading the word about the product?" Greg clarified.

"No…not all of them. Only our best clients are invited in on that kind of deal," Pete said.

"So, I'm one of your best clients?" Matt looked incredulous.

"Yes." Pete smiled.

"Even though I haven't bought anything yet." Matt frowned.

"Well…er…" Pete looked flummoxed.

"But we're confident you're going to," Dan interjected. "After all, you wouldn't have come all this way for nothing, would you?"

"And yet you haven't discussed a price." Tom was the last to stand.

"Look…er…How about we take this over to the bar? Discuss it properly over a real drink?" Pete suggested.

"But the only thing we need to discuss are testimonials and cost," Matt said, sounding a little irate.

"And you don't seem keen to divulge either right now," Greg pointed out.

"Yeah, and we need to be heading back," Matt said.

"Oh, right. We don't normally rush these things," Pete gushed. "But if you're in a hurry…"

"Yeah." Matt's voice was clipped.

"Here." Dan offered him a sheet of paper. "All the prices are on there."

"And testimonials?" Tom asked.

"They're on the website." Dan almost spat the words at him.

"No, we mean ones we can see results of with our own eyes…in person," Matt replied. "Don't you have anyone willing to show us the effects this product has had on their cattle? Apart from the pictures on your website, of course."

"Here. Ring this guy," Dan said, taking back one of the papers he'd just handed to Matt. "This is Ben Hathaway, a local farmer. Uses the supplements all the time. I'm sure he'd be only too happy to speak to you about his excellent results." He jotted down the number and handed the paper back.

"Thank you." Matt glanced at it. "Is that a four or a seven?" He pointed to one of the figures.

"Seven," Dan replied, without even looking at it.

"Thanks again." Matt shook their hands.

"We look forward to hearing from you," Pete said, pasting on a fake smile.

"Well, if this stuff's as good as you say it is – and the price is right – I'd be a fool not to give it a try." Matt's smile looked sickly, and Tom knew his boss was annoyed.

"My condolences again, about your wife," Tom said, as he shook Dan's hand.

"Is she ill, then?" Greg glanced over.

"What? Savannah?" Pete looked stunned, gaping at Dan. She looked fine last time I..."

"Thank you," Dan snapped, before ushering them all toward the door.

It was hard to tell who was the most relieved to get out of there, but it was no surprise to Tom to watch Pete and Dan head quickly in the direction of what he could only assume was the local bar.

Chapter Eight

Savannah lay alone in her room, her mind spinning with confusion and worry. This should all have been so simple. She should have been able to just walk out the front door and start her journey. Surely someone driving past would have offered her a ride, at least to the nearest town. But the throb in her ankle reminded her that she couldn't walk. And she'd hardly seen any traffic on that back road the other night when she'd arrived.

So, here she was, stuck in a very nice guest house with three very nice people. But she didn't feel nice. She'd lied to these people—and not the sort of lies that pacified her husband, telling him just what he wanted to hear. These were ugly lies, the sort she despised and never told.

She sighed, lying on one side facing the open window. Birds sang outside and every now then she could hear the faint mooing of cattle. Occasionally a vehicle would rattle up the street, and there was a low murmur of chattering from passers-by. Pelican's Heath was alive, not like Upton Crossing.

Her home was a small cottage near the railway line that gave the town its name. Several times a day a train would thunder down the rickety track, making it shake and objects rattle and fall from shelves. In between trains was silence, which made the railway seem even noisier each time it sprang into action.

She couldn't decide which she hated more — the sound of nothingness or the racket of the trains. Imagining herself back in that house, cleaning all day and cooking for an ungrateful husband made her feel even more down. Why would she want to go back to that?

It hadn't occurred to her before today that she'd actually gotten what she wanted. She'd gotten away. Daniel didn't want her. She had nothing to go back to. Okay, so her clothes were there, but she didn't have anything of any value. Daniel had seen to that. He'd sold her jewelry — apart from one tiny bracelet she kept hidden — and her late mother's silver to help with the deposit for the house. The house *he* had chosen. The one he had paid for, and she could lay no claim to, not that she'd want to.

"Ah, you're awake." Mrs. Hodges sounded cheerful.

Savannah rolled around to face her. "Sorry. I… I don't know what happened. I just felt a bit…"

"It's all right, dear. You just passed out. I called the doctor and he said it was probably exertion. You shouldn't have been out of bed, really. Here… I've brought you some coffee and cake. You missed lunch. Can I get you some soup or perhaps some bread and cheese?"

Savannah shook her head, scooting up into a sitting position. "No, thank you. Cake will be fine. I love your homemade cakes."

Mrs. Hodges beamed at the compliment. "Thank you. I'd be glad to share the recipe if you…"

"Would you? That would be wonderful!" Savannah imagined herself in Mrs. Hodges' kitchen, helping her bake for her guests. She'd love that.

"I'm sorry you couldn't go home," Mrs. Hodges said, sitting down in the little chair. "The boys couldn't take you in that state and it wouldn't be safe to leave you on your own like that, anyway."

Savannah nodded, more relieved than disappointed. "They're very kind. You all are."

"Maybe in a few days they'll be able to take you back? When you're stronger." Mrs. Hodges smiled.

"Maybe," Savannah agreed. "In the meantime, it looks like you're stuck with me."

The older lady laughed. "Don't be silly. I'm enjoying having some female company for a change. It's usually just businessmen that take my rooms, and even then, not usually long enough for me to get to know them."

"Have Tom and Greg been here long?" Savannah asked before taking another bite of the delicious fruit cake.

"A couple of months, nearly. They took a room when they first got taken on at the Shearer Ranch. They're going to rent a house on the outskirts of Pelican's Heath, near to Bracken Ridge. The landlord Jack Purslow's just having the place redecorated. It should be ready in a few days' time." Mrs. Hodges looked a little sad.

"You'll miss them, won't you?"

"I will," she admitted, "though I'll still have other folks staying here by then. I'm expecting some business from the Fieldings soon. They own the large ranch that takes up most of the land around these parts. There's going to be a big party for Josie's birthday, and they can't accommodate everyone over there, so they're going to send a few guests my way."

"That's handy," Savannah remarked.

"It'll be hard work," Mrs. Hodges replied, "but it'll be fun."

"Do you employ extra help when you've got more guests?" Savannah asked.

"No. I should, I suppose. It would make life easier." Mrs. Hodges looked thoughtful.

"I'd be glad to help." Savannah's response was automatic and even surprised herself.

"You'll have better things to do by then," Mrs. Hodges said with a smile. "It's a week or so yet. You'll be back home and not giving us folks a second thought."

Savannah's stomach lurched at the idea. She couldn't go home. And, she realized, she didn't want to leave them. She liked it here, and she enjoyed the company of the old lady and the handsome cowboys. In fact, she was concerned that she was enjoying those guys' company a little too much.

Mrs. Hodges wiped crumbs from her wrinkled face and placed her plate back on the tray. Her hands trembled as she lifted her cup and saucer. She absent-mindedly wiped a curl from her cheek before taking a sip of her drink.

"Let me do your hair for you," Savannah offered, in a flash of inspiration. "I learned hairdressing. I used to be quite good at it." She smiled at the memory. She'd gotten her qualifications and had hoped to run her own salon one day.

"Really?" Mrs. Hodges looked surprised.

Savannah nodded. "I won a competition once for best bridal hair. My model looked absolutely lovely. I added little wisps of gypsophila around her curls, and she had all this hair up at the back, with tendrils all down here." She showed her with her own hair, lifting it up and pulling little strands down. "It wasn't easy, mind you," she recalled. "The poor girl got caught in the rain on the way to the event, and her hair was all frizzy. I had to tame it before I could do anything with it. I was afraid I'd run out of time, but it was okay."

"You sound very proud. I'd have loved to have seen it." Mrs. Hodges smiled.

"I had a photo of it…" She suddenly remembered that the photo was in a file at home, under the bed, somewhere she probably wouldn't be returning to. "But I think it got ruined when we had a burst pipe. Water went everywhere," she added.

"Oh, no, that must have been awful!" Mrs. Hodges looked so sympathetic that Savannah felt guilty for fibbing.

"Shall I put some rollers in for you?" she asked, trying to hide her shame.

"That would be lovely, if you're sure you're well enough, dear? I usually go to the salon but I just haven't had time."

"There's a hair salon in Pelican's Heath?"

"Yes. It's small, only one hairdresser. She does manicures, too, but only when she's not too busy with hair."

"I can do manicures. I'll do yours." Savannah suddenly became much more positive. She'd loved working as a hairdresser and had been devastated when, just after their wedding, Daniel had announced that she was to give up work and concentrate on cleaning the house. He expected certain standards in his home and, apparently, she hadn't been reaching them. He'd thought that giving up work would allow her more time to devote to being a *proper* wife.

* * * *

"Well, that was interesting," Tom said as they clambered back into Matt's truck.

"I got the impression they were more interested in making money *off* me than *from* me," Matt said.

"That figures. Dan more or less propositioned me in the bathroom," Tom said.

Greg stared at him. "You mean he's gay?"

"Ha-ha. Very funny. I mean he was asking if I wanted to make a few extra bucks selling the stuff for him." Tom rolled his eyes.

Greg let out a long breath, more relieved than he cared to admit.

"Take a look at those papers," Matt told Greg, who was sitting in the middle of the bench seat. "There should be a number on there for this Hathaway guy."

"You believe that?" Greg looked surprised as he reached for the shelf under the dashboard where his boss had left the paperwork.

"Nope." Matt grinned. "But it might be fun to find out what they're playing at. I thought we might ring this guy and ask if we can drop in on our way home, take a look at his cattle. It'll be interesting to see what excuse he comes up with."

"I like the way you think, boss." Greg chuckled.

"Let me just take a look at the number first," Tom said, leaning over.

He pulled Dan's card from his pocket and compared the digits with the ones scribbled on the back of a form.

"Hmm, just a thought. He could have given us his own number."

"Pete Bramhall's is in my cell," Matt said. "Check it out."

Greg took the phone from him and scrolled down to find the number. It didn't match.

"Better give it a ring, then, I reckon," Matt said, pulling over to the side of the road.

He rang the number and was disappointed, though hardly surprised, when his call went straight through to voicemail.

"Hi there, I'm looking to speak to a Mr. Ben Hathaway," he said in a cheerful tone. "My name's Matt Shearer and I'm very interested in purchasing a large batch of feed nutrients from Stone Supplements over at Upton. Pete Bramhall and Dan Edgerton suggested I call you to see what you thought of their products. I was hoping to stop by and take a look at your cattle, if that's okay, to see how effective the nutrients are. I'll look forward to hearing from you as soon as you can, as I desperately need to save my herd." He left his number and chuckled as soon as he'd ended the call. "That should get 'em going."

"I'd say," Greg said, with a whistle. "Have you seen the cost of this stuff? Those guys must be making a mint!"

"No wonder they weren't keen to give you a price without a few stiff drinks inside you," Tom said, peering over Greg's shoulder.

"Hmm, something sure smells off about all this," Matt said, shaking his head.

"I was afraid for a second back there that you were actually considering doing business with these schmucks," Tom admitted.

Matt raised his eyebrows indignantly. "Do I *look* stupid?"

"Well, you were putting on a good act, boss," Tom replied with a grin.

"I just know that my brother will want as much information as he can get on them," he said.

Tom and Greg exchanged a look.

"About that..." Greg chewed his lip.

"Dyson?"

"Yeah. I mentioned Savannah to him yesterday. I probably shouldn't have said anything. Looks like she might be in some kind of trouble and any questions from the sheriff could make things even worse for her." Greg's face went hot.

"I'm sure he'll be discreet, guys," Matt replied with a smile. "Bit of a coincidence that guy losing his wife recently, what with having the same name and all."

"Why the fuck would you claim your wife's dead?" Tom said through gritted teeth.

"So no one'll go looking for her?" Greg suggested.

"That guy really needs to get his story straight. Even his partner had no idea what he was saying about her." Matt grinned. "Nice one, landing him in it like that, Tom. I admire your style, man."

Tom looked over in surprise. "Just couldn't resist it."

"Maybe we should've gone to the bar with them?" Greg suggested. "I'd have loved to see him get out of that one."

They all chuckled.

"Still begs the question about what happened with Savannah," Greg mused. "Was she running away from him, do you think?"

"If she was, I'd like to know the reason why. A woman doesn't just leave her home in the middle of the night without so much as a coat, then walk all that way in a storm." Tom sounded angry.

"So, what's she told you guys? Surely, she must have given some kind of explanation?" Matt asked, frowning.

"She went looking for her dog," Greg said.

"Well, there's no doubt that's untrue," Tom said, with a grimace. "No way would that fucker have let her keep a pet."

"I guess one animal in the house is enough," Greg muttered.

"Aw, come on, guys. You don't know this guy did anything wrong. Why not wait until we've got a few facts before you go jumping to conclusions, eh?" Matt shook his head.

"Well, she must have had a really good reason to lie to us." Tom stared out of the window, clearly deep in thought.

"Yeah, like none of us has ever lied," Greg chided. "Or even just neglected to tell the truth?"

"That's different," Tom said. "We don't know her well enough yet. No point in putting her off right from the start, is there?"

"I still think you judge yourself much more harshly than anyone else does," Matt offered.

Tom sighed.

"You really like this girl, don't you, guys?" Matt went on. "Well, if you want my advice, I think you all need to talk to one another. Find out exactly how the ground lies. She might have a perfectly reasonable explanation."

"Well, we've just seen how her husband lies," Tom said with a sigh. "I'd sure like that fucker to explain why he's claiming his wife's dead."

"Maybe he believes she is," Greg suggested.

Chapter Nine

"Wow… I hardly recognized you, Mrs. H," Greg teased when the guys arrived home that evening.

The older lady blushed. "Savannah did my hair and nails," she explained, showing them her hands. She had very pale pink nail polish on and had gotten a good manicure.

"Very nice." Greg nodded his approval. "Where is she?" He peered from the kitchen into the living room but here was no sign of her. His breath hitched. *Surely, she hasn't left?*

"She's in bed. I think it exhausted her, doing all this, though it was great fun. She said she was feeling tired and just had a sandwich for supper. Said she wasn't that hungry."

Greg frowned. "She should eat."

"Is she a hairdresser, then?" Tom asked.

"Yeah. Does nails, too. I reckon she could get a job with Sandy over at the salon if she didn't live so dang far away."

The guys exchanged a look.

"Maybe she'd like to move over here?" Greg suggested.

"Yeah, she could work for Sandy and stay with us. We should have the house soon." Tom looked quite hopeful and Greg did his best to suppress his own enthusiasm.

"Only if she wanted to," he said.

Mrs. Hodges chuckled. "Guys, you're not forgetting that husband of hers, are you? And she might even have children, for all we know. It might not be so easy to move all the way out here, even if she could get a job."

Greg's stomach lurched. Savannah couldn't go home even if she wanted to, by the looks of things, but he couldn't tell Mrs. Hodges that. His gut roiled with anger at how her husband had spoken about her, and he cringed at the thought that Savannah might have faked her own death to get away from him. Tom hadn't believed his theory, saying that the guy was definitely a phony — and Greg had to concede that his buddy had spent more time with Daniel than any of them — but he couldn't help wondering if he was right.

"We'd best get cleaned up," Tom said, turning back toward the kitchen door.

"Supper'll be on the table in ten minutes," Mrs. Hodges promised.

"It would be great if she could move over this way," Greg murmured as they passed Savannah's bedroom door. There was silence from inside and he was desperate to go in and see if she was all right.

"It's a fair way from Upton Crossing," Tom replied. "I just hope it's far enough."

Savannah had lain stock-still as she heard the guys pass her room. Her breath hitched when she heard Greg's comment and she hoped he was talking about her. Would they really want her to move here?

She'd told Mrs. Hodges she wasn't that hungry this evening, though the lady had insisted she have at least a ham sandwich for supper. The guys were a little late getting home and Savannah had welcomed the opportunity to get to bed before they arrived. She couldn't tolerate any more of their questions tonight.

Her mind whirred as she closed her eyes. She liked those guys a lot. Too much, maybe. Both were gorgeous, although very different. Mrs. Hodges has said earlier that Frankie had been their girlfriend. They liked to share. She'd never even considered a ménage relationship before, but there was no way she could choose between those guys, so it was the perfect option in this case.

She guessed that Greg would be a lot of fun in the bedroom. The way his eyes twinkled suggested he'd be quite adventurous. Her stomach roiled a little at the thought. Daniel would never entertain the idea of doing anything but missionary position. In his view, anything else was kinky and only for freaks.

She'd read in magazines and in the books she'd devoured while Daniel was at work about women having a much better time than her. He'd have thrown her out a lot sooner if he'd known that she harbored ideas about doggy-style and oral sex. Until now, those thoughts had only been fantasies, unattainable dreams. Her heart beat a little faster at the notion that maybe – just maybe – that sort of thing was possible for her.

Greg would be a gentle lover, coaxing and caring. He would make suggestions with a certain look, the raise of an eyebrow, the wink of an eye. His reassuring smile would give her confidence to try new things. Her mouth watered as she imagined what he'd look like naked. He was strong, and she'd felt his biceps through his shirt. He wouldn't have much chest hair, as he was so fair, but he probably had a buff six-pack. He had the confidence of a guy who would be well hung and she imagined he would know plenty of ways to please a girl.

He would give her a long, lingering kiss, the sort that she would feel right down to her groin. She'd never been kissed like that but she'd read about it and longed to experience it. Daniel's lips were thin and tight, and they'd seldom kissed.

Greg would stroke her willing body with his big hands, making her shiver and moan. His voice would be soft and encouraging, and she would just know that anything she did with him would be okay. She wouldn't be mocked for wanting to be touched in a certain place or told she was frigid for not wanting to do something. Rolling onto her stomach, she imagined Greg stroking her pussy. It would be wet. That was how it should be when people had sex. She would be ready, for once. Greg's massive cock would slowly enter her, stretching her with delicious strength, molding her to his shape. He would find that special spot that only she'd ever touched. His scent would surround her in a cloud of euphoria, and his body would encompass hers. He would talk to her, encouraging her and empowering her. His body would meld with hers and his cock would stroke all her nerve endings. His heavy balls would press against her butt with every stroke, and he wouldn't stop teasing her breasts and flicking at her pussy. She would come in a wave of ecstasy, screaming out her orgasm for the first time ever as his hot seed would gush into her, accompanied by his guttural roar of pleasure.

She clutched her pillow, imagining him enveloping her with gentle arms and pulling her into his chest as their hearts hammered and their panting slowed.

Tom seemed a lot quieter than Greg, and she found his eyes quite mysterious and engaging. He conveyed a lot with his expressions, and she imagined he was much more sensitive than he'd care to admit. He had been devastated when he had almost knocked her over that first night, and he'd seemed so apologetic afterward.

His smoldering eyes would be enough to coax her out of her clothes, and she imagined he would use few words to convey his intentions, not that that would be a problem.

Although he didn't appear quite as confident as Greg, she got the impression he would be quite assertive in bed. He would want to make love to her looking into her eyes. She had already seen that his chest had a scattering of hair and an abundance of muscle. His body would be like iron, though not cold. He would crawl up the bed toward her, watching her expression throughout. She would shiver with anticipation and hope as he crept over her body, like a panther stalking its prey. His brooding eyes would become darker and he'd open his mouth slightly, though he wouldn't speak.

She'd rolled onto her back again and imagined his heaving body covering hers. Just watching him would make her pussy ache for his touch, her nipples harden and her hopes rise.

He would gaze into her face, something she wasn't used to, but would welcome from him. Studying her, he would read every nuance, every expression, and would feel her need.

Tom would be a slow, careful lover. His huge cock would enter her only when she was silently begging for his touch, when she couldn't wait a second longer. He would take her slowly but thoroughly, as her pussy would swallow him whole, yielding to his massive girth and relishing his strength. He would heave in and out of her soaking pussy, lighting up nerves she never knew existed, introducing her to new feelings and sensations.

He wouldn't come until she had, and she would scream his name as he commanded her to look at him while he sent her over the edge. His stare would burn into her and his pleasure would be palpable. He would groan his elation as his seed would explode into her womb.

Savannah suddenly opened her eyes. A sound had woken her, and she was afraid it was of her own making. Had she actually screamed Tom's name? She stared at the door, straining her ears for the sound of movement from downstairs. What if they all came rushing in? Would her panting breath and flushed body betray her?

She wanted to run to the bathroom and have a cool wash, but her body wouldn't move. It *couldn't* move. She was pinned to the bed by the fear of exposure.

Quickly wiping her sweating face in the pillow, she reached out for the glass of water on the nightstand. It wasn't as cold as she needed, but it helped cool her a little. She forced her breathing to slow, still looking at the door, daring it to open.

Her breath hitched as she thought she heard a sound. A gulp of water tickled her throat and she coughed, replacing the glass. The drink had gone down the wrong way and she choked, panic-stricken. Tears filled her eyes as she fought for an unattainable breath.

She didn't see the door burst open or the concern in the guys' eyes as they ran over to the bed. She felt Greg's warm arm around her and heard Tom's soothing voice.

"What is it?" Tom asked.

She pointed to the water.

"Water?"

She nodded, already beginning to gulp in some air. The terror that had engulfed her dissipated, just knowing they were there.

"Deep breaths, Savannah," Tom instructed in a composed, gentle tone.

Greg patted her back then wiped the tears from her eyes as she slowly managed to breathe.

"Take your time," Tom soothed as he gradually came into focus. He was kneeling on the floor in front of her, watching her face.

Greg was sitting next to her on the bed, his arm still around her back. He handed her a tissue.

"Thank you," she whispered. "I'm sorry. I just couldn't catch my breath."

"You sure got yourself into a state," Tom said, his own face relaxing.

Savannah's face became hotter.

"A trickle of water went down the wrong way, huh?" Greg asked with a grin.

She nodded, feeling more than a little foolish. "I'm sorry. I didn't mean to worry you guys."

"Of course we worried, dear. We care about you." Mrs. Hodges was standing by the door, taking Savannah by surprise.

She stared over at the old woman, who was silhouetted by the hallway light shining through the open door behind her.

"You're very kind," she croaked. "All of you."

Greg gave her a gentle squeeze before offering her the glass of water. "Hair of the dog that bit ya?" He beamed.

A warmth flooded Savannah's stomach. She nodded, taking the drink, which she sipped very slowly. She could sense them all watching her, as though expecting her to start choking again.

"Thank you." She gave the glass back to Greg with a sigh of relief.

In the calm aftermath, she glanced at the guys, who were every bit as handsome as they'd been in her dream. She blushed, hoping they couldn't read her mind.

"Do you need anything?" Tom asked.

"No, I'm fine now. Thank you." She really wanted to use the bathroom but wasn't about to reveal that to them. "I'm just sorry for disturbing you all."

"Actually, we were about to go to bed," Greg told her. "But Tom thought he heard his name called just before we realized you were choking."

"It was really good of you to check on me," she replied.

"Anytime, sweetheart." Greg kissed the top of her head before standing up.

"Goodnight, Savannah," Tom said, his dark eyes boring into her.

A sobering thought crossed her mind as she watched him follow Greg and Mrs. Hodges out the door. *He knows.*

"That girl sure can blush," Greg whispered as he climbed into bed.

Tom stifled a grin. He knew what he'd heard and he'd seen how flustered Savannah was as soon as he'd opened the door. It wasn't all down to a trickle of water. He was certain of that, though he accepted it was a contributing factor.

"She's not used to people caring about her. That's for sure," he murmured back. He was already in his bed, one foot over the top of his covers and an arm behind his head.

"It's not hard to see why." Greg snorted.

"We can't tell her we know about her husband."

Greg agreed, "Do you think she knows she can't go home, though? She seemed pretty keen to head back there this morning."

"Or was she just in a hurry to leave?" Tom wondered.

"D'you think she's got someplace to go?"

He shook his head. "If she had any friends or relatives who could take her in, she would've contacted them by now. Mrs. Hodges said she hasn't mentioned anyone except her husband, who she's maintaining is away."

"Hmm. Uncontactable, you mean." Greg frowned. "It's a pity she couldn't just come right on out and tell us the truth. He's a bastard and she's getting away from him."

"That would be admitting defeat," Tom replied. "And no one wants to do that."

"Sorry, buddy." Greg looked like he was about to kick himself. "I didn't mean…"

"I know."

Tom clicked off the light and they fell silent, though he wasn't ready for sleep just yet. The vision of Savannah's beautiful, flushed face haunted him, and he heard her calling his name over and over. Not in a frantic, scared tone, but in the desperate, needy way of a woman out of control with desire. The thought warmed him right through. She was beautiful, and despite Greg's claim that she was off-limits, he couldn't stop his heart from hoping.

Savannah was nothing like Beth Coulter. Beth had been blonde with pale blue eyes and had been shy and quiet. Savannah's fiery red hair matched her temperament. She was strong-willed and had a mind of her own. Her big, green eyes flashed when she was annoyed and he could imagine her getting mad. He found her exciting and knew she was frustrated that she wasn't as physically strong as she'd have liked. Beth had been sweet and fragile and he'd just wanted to look after her all the time — but he hadn't. That was the trouble.

Chapter Ten

The next few days passed slowly for Savannah. She kept to herself as much as she could when the guys were home. Mrs. Hodges insisted that she stay in bed as much as possible while she recovered from that awful cold, and her ankle gradually healed.

Having her meals in her room prevented her having to negotiate the stairs, which saved Mrs. Hodges a lot of worry, and Savannah was glad to not have to answer all the awkward questions the guys seemed to enjoy firing at her over the meal table.

She became shy whenever Tom or Greg popped into her room to say hi, although she loved seeing them, which was the problem. Tom had a way of peering right into her soul whenever he looked at her, and she found herself excited but unnerved by it. *Is he actually a mind reader?*

Greg was more easy-going and flirtatious, and both guys' lighthearted banter had her in fits of giggles. They seemed to love poking fun at each other, which surprised and delighted Savannah. It reminded her how serious her life had gotten lately.

"How are those poor cattle now?" she asked on the third evening when they had all congregated in her room for a catch-up.

"They're doing really well," Greg told her with a smile. He was sprawled on her bed next to her with an arm around her shoulder. It had become his usual position and she loved it. "The pasture out here's so good that they've managed without anything extra."

Relief swept through her. She had dreaded them asking for the details of Daniel's company for those feed supplements.

"Why don't you come and see for yourself?" Tom piped up from the armchair. "We've got the day off tomorrow, so we could take you over and introduce you to everyone. Carla would love to meet you. She keeps asking how you are."

"Hey, great idea. We could show you around Pelican's Heath, too. You haven't seen the town yet, have you?" Greg squeezed her shoulder.

"Now, don't you go running before you can walk — literally." Mrs. Hodges came in carrying a tray of tea and homemade cookies that she plunked on the nightstand.

"I thought the doc said her ankle was much better?" Tom queried, standing up to offer the old lady his seat. "It might do her good to take a gentle stroll. And the fresh air could put some color into her cheeks."

Mrs. Hodges sat down with a sigh, looking over at Savannah thoughtfully. "True," she conceded with a nod. "It'll give me a chance to air this room and get some shopping in for next week, too."

"Yeah, and maybe we could take a trip over to Bracken Ridge and show her our new place," Greg added.

Savannah was acutely aware that the guys would be moving out of the bed-and-breakfast over the next few days. Their new home was now redecorated and ready for them to move into, and Mrs. Hodges was making plans to let their rooms out to some of the Fieldings' friends who were coming over for a party at the family ranch. The thought of the guys not being there any longer saddened her and also reminded her that she needed to think about moving on, too.

"We could take the first of our stuff over with us," Tom said, pouring out the tea.

"I'd like to see where you're going to live," Savannah said, taking the cup from him.

"You'll need to wrap up warm," Mrs. Hodges warned.

"We'll lend her some of our stuff," Greg offered, tucking into a large chocolate-chip cookie. Savannah smiled. She loved borrowing the guys' clothes, even though they were far too big for her, and she looked forward to them showing her around the town. She'd met a few of the locals already. Mrs. Taylor, whose daughter owned a clothes shop, was a good friend of Mrs. Hodges and had popped in for coffee on a couple of occasions, and the doctor dropped by almost every day. She'd heard someone delivering groceries, too, who'd stayed for some lunch while she was holed up in her room, and the mailman sounded cheerful.

While her window was open, she'd heard people chattering and laughing in the street below and had sensed a positive vibe. This seemed like the sort of place she'd always wanted to live, not stuck out in the middle of nowhere on her own for days on end.

"We'd best let you get some rest, then," Mrs. Hodges said, gathering up the cups a short while later. "It sounds like you've got a busy day ahead tomorrow. You'll need all your strength."

Savannah snuggled down under the covers as they all left the room. Greg had kissed her on the head again tonight, and Tom had winked on his way out of the door. She was having the most inappropriate thoughts about those handsome hunks and was dangerously close to never wanting to leave them. But how could she stick around now that they knew she was already married? What would people think? And what about Daniel?

* * * *

The winter sun was straining through the gap in the drapes when Savannah awoke the next morning. She felt positive and hopeful. It was a joy to get out of bed and take a shower, after removing the support bandage on her ankle. Putting her weight on her right foot no longer sent pains shooting through her, and she was able to pull her jeans on without gritting her teeth, for once.

Her battered sneakers wouldn't last much longer, and her sweater was totally out of shape now, as it hung like a rag over her body. It was all she had, though, apart from some new underwear that Mrs. Hodges had kindly bought her a few days ago.

"Good morning, beautiful." Tom greeted her with a smile as soon as she opened her bedroom door to go downstairs. "How are you feeling?"

She beamed at him. "Much better, thanks. I'm looking forward to getting out today."

"We thought we'd head over to Bracken Ridge first, show you our new place," he explained, holding her arm as she slowly took one stair at a time. "We've packed some of our stuff, so we'll drop it over there."

She nodded. "I can't wait to see it. Is it far?"

"Just on the outskirts of Pelican's Heath."

The smell of bacon and sausages welcomed them into the kitchen, where Mrs. Hodges was busy at the stove, while Greg was just coming in through the back door, rubbing his hands.

"It's cold out there," he said, before looking over and noticing them. "Hey, you're up. How are you today?"

"I'm fine, thanks," Tom replied, cheekily. "It's good of you to ask, bro."

Greg rolled his eyes. "Very funny. I was actually talking to Savannah."

She giggled as Tom put a hand over his chest.

"Well, I'm mortally wounded," he said, letting his bottom lip droop.

"Yeah, I'll bet you are." Greg shook his head.

"When you boys have quite finished, your breakfast's ready," Mrs. Hodges held out a plate full of bacon, sausages, eggs and beans.

"Lovely!" Greg enthused, taking the plate from her.

"How come he gets his first?" Tom whined as the lady dished up another three platefuls.

"Well, in the first place, I'm the one who just took the trash out, so at least I've been making myself useful this morning. And in the second place, it's not for me. It's for Savannah." Greg placed the food on the table before pulling out a chair for her.

"Thank you," she said, sitting down with a smile. She started to blush as he leaned over her, surrounding her in his fresh scent as he placed a napkin on her lap.

Tom narrowed his eyes at his buddy but said nothing. He helped Mrs. Hodges bring over the rest of the meals and they all sat down to eat.

"How many rooms do you have here?" Savannah asked, wondering where everyone would sit to eat if the place became even busier. There were four of them sitting around the kitchen table and it already looked full.

"Four, though one's usually just used for storage," Mrs. Hodges replied. "Only one has the en suite bathroom, though."

"That's our room," Tom said, reaching for some toast.

"It's the biggest. The others are singles." Mrs. Hodges wiped the crumbs from her mouth. "Looks like I'll be using all of them next week. The Fieldings are having a lot of guests over for Josie's party."

"We'll be out of your hair in a couple of days," Greg assured her with a grin.

"Oh, I wasn't hinting." The old lady looked flustered.

"I know. But you'll need the space." Greg smiled at her.

Savannah's stomach lurched. She needed to move out and give Mrs. Hodges back that room she was staying in. She wasn't even paying, for goodness' sake, and despite her promise to reimburse the old lady for her board, she had no way of getting an income yet.

"It's freezing outside," Greg pointed out as they ate. "Do you wanna borrow some boots, Savannah? And I've got a thicker sweater than that, if you need it?"

"That's a good idea." Mrs. Hodges nodded. "You'll need a jacket, too. We don't want you going back down with that awful cold. It's taken this long to beat it."

"You can have my spare Carhartt," Tom offered.

"That's really kind of you," she said with a smile. She'd been dreading going out looking like such a wreck in her old clothes.

After breakfast they said goodbye to Mrs. Hodges and piled into the pickup. Greg had already loaded some boxes into the back, and they headed out of town.

Bracken Ridge was a small area, with just a few houses, a motel, post office and a very run-down café.

"It's not the liveliest of places, is it?" Greg said with a grin as they pulled up outside a large house.

"We like it quiet," Tom explained. "We're the sort of folks who like to keep ourselves to ourselves."

Savannah smiled as Greg helped her down from her seat. The birds were chirping and cows could be heard somewhere in the distance.

"It's not completely deserted," Greg assured her. He pointed up the road. "There are more houses over that way a little."

"I think it's lovely," she said. "And you've got a café practically on your doorstep."

Tom snorted. "I don't know how long for. The guy that owns it is a miserable cuss and can't cook for toffee. Maggie Fielding used to work there, apparently, but Carla said that since she left, the place has gone completely downhill."

"That's a shame." Savannah helped take the boxes from the back of the truck and followed the guys into the house. It would be nice to put faces to the names the guys talked about.

"Wow, this is huge!" She gasped as soon as she got inside.

"Glad you like it," Greg said with a grin. "Just dump those anywhere."

They'd entered through the front door and she could smell fresh paint in the air. The ceiling was high and she followed the guys through the hall into a vast living room.

"It'll probably look smaller when we get some furniture," Tom said, rubbing his arms after placing his load in a pile by the door. "Perhaps you could help us pick some out?"

Savannah's heart lurched. She'd adore having a hand in making this their home and just wished she could afford a place like it.

"I'd love to."

"Great. We've already got the bedrooms furnished, but we'll need something to sit on down here," Greg piped up.

"And you'll need drapes at those windows," she pointed out. "That'll be one of the first things to get, I expect."

"She's got a point there, bro." Tom pouted. "We don't want any nosey pokes spying on us."

"Ha! Like who? There's no one around, in case you hadn't noticed." Greg chuckled.

"And that's just how I like it," Tom replied.

"But surely you'd want some company sometimes?" Savannah was reminded of her home in Upton Crossing and how lonely she'd been, being so far from anyone else.

"Yup. That's why we're living so close to Pelican's Heath," Greg told her. "We get to have the best of both worlds—the hustle and bustle of town but the peace and quiet when we get home."

Savannah smiled. That sounded like a good compromise, and one she'd be glad of herself, given the choice.

"And talking of town, we'd best head off," Tom said.

They climbed back into the truck, Savannah sandwiched between the two hunks. Tom drove again, and she gazed at his tan arms as they stretched across the steering wheel. His sweater sleeves had ridden up and she could see his muscles ripple.

Greg had his arm around the back of the seat, cradling her as he toyed with her hair. He was very tactile, and although she wasn't used to it, she enjoyed feeling him so close.

"We'll show you around the town first, then we can go over to the ranch and introduce you to the Shearers," Tom said.

"I think Carla might be working at the shop this morning," Greg said. He turned to Savannah. "She works part-time in the local store, as well as helping at the ranch."

She nodded. The guys were clearly fond of the family they worked for, and she longed to be part of a community like this.

Tom parked at the side of the road and Greg helped her out of the truck again. She loved feeling his strong arms reach up and hold her, and her body brushed against his as she reached the ground. Her fear that he would let her go as soon as she was safely on terra firma dissipated as he casually slung an arm around her shoulder.

"This is much busier than I imagined," she said, looking around at the shops.

"Not as busy as Almondine," Tom said, coming to join them, "I really wouldn't want to live there."

"Where's Mrs. Hodges' house?" She peered up the street but nothing looked familiar. She didn't even know what the house looked like from the outside, but she'd noticed a large tree opposite her bedroom window and had seen the street below.

"Down the street and around the corner," Greg explained. "She doesn't live in the busiest part. It's a little quieter back there."

"Come on. We'll show you around," Tom offered, throwing his arm over her shoulder, too. There was a small diner across the street and a few tiny shops.

"This is where Carla works," Greg said, as they neared a general store.

They went in and she was surprised how small it was. It was very neatly laid out and incredibly clean. Rows of shelves selling anything from moccasins to macaroons led up to the main counter, where a pretty girl with long, dark hair was smiling at them.

"Hey, Carla, this is Savannah." Greg introduced them while Carla rushed around the side of the counter.

"Hi, Savannah. It's so lovely to meet you. The guys haven't stopped talking about you all week. How are you?" She gave Savannah a hug.

"I'm fine, thank you." Savannah went warm inside. She'd never been made so welcome in her life — and this woman was a perfect stranger. "Just a bit of a cold left, but I'm much better."

"I hope these guys have been looking after you," Carla said, looking up at the men.

"Yeah, they've been wonderful." Savannah blushed.

"We're just showing her around town," Tom said. "She hasn't been out of that guest house the whole time she's been here."

Carla looked surprised. "You must be going stir-crazy!"

Savannah smiled, not wishing to explain that at home she'd often spent several days holed up in her house, not allowed to take so much as a short walk because Daniel was in one of his moods.

"She does hair," Greg offered. "We thought we'd introduce her to Sandy at the salon."

Carla's eyes lit up. "Well, if you're planning on sticking around, you could make a lot of money as a *mobile* hairdresser," she said. "Sandy's rushed off her feet and some of us don't get much chance to get into town during working hours when it's busy on the ranch. You could go around and cut folks' hair in their homes."

Savannah's heart raced as much as her mind at the idea. She would love to do something like that.

"Yeah, and you could do their nails, too," Greg added, his eyes twinkling.

"I don't drive," Savannah said, remembering with crushing disappointment that being mobile would be a large part of the job.

"We can teach you," Greg said. Although he grinned at her, she noticed him and Tom exchange a worried look. She'd picked up on that expression before, several times.

"Are you going up to the ranch?" Carla asked.

"Yeah, we just wanted to introduce Savannah to everyone," Tom said.

"It's Dyson's day off. They'll be pleased to see you." She smiled at Savannah, whose stomach roiled at the sound of the sheriff's name. She wasn't so sure that he'd be all that happy to see her after their last encounter.

"We'll just show her around the shops first, then we'll head on over there," Greg said.

They said goodbye to Carla and made their way back up the street.

"Down that way's a great boutique you might like," Tom pointed out, indicating a side street. "All the women are raving about it."

"I'll take a look some time," she said, feeling sick to her stomach that she couldn't afford any new clothes. She'd had to borrow an extra couple of pairs of Greg's socks to fit his boots, although his sweater and Tom's jacket were really comfy, being so roomy.

"The salon's this way." Greg steered her back across the street.

This, again, was a much smaller business than she had envisaged, and she was surprised at how many ladies were packed into the tiny room. They were all chatting happily, and a large woman was combing conditioner through an elderly lady's hair at the backwash.

"Hey, guys. You back already?" The lady came over to them, smiling.

"Hi, Sandy. We're not here for a cut, thank goodness. Looks like you've got enough business to keep you going 'til midnight." Greg put an arm around her for a hug, and Savannah experienced a twinge of jealousy, not the least because she was a pretty woman with bright red lipstick and her dark hair was in the kind of neat bun Savannah could only dream of.

"It *is* busy," Sandy agreed, before putting an arm out for Tom.

"Well, we might be able to help you out, there," Tom said, after a quick cuddle. "We'd like you to meet a good friend of ours, Savannah Edgerton. She does hair and nails. We thought maybe you could use an extra pair of hands around the place?"

Savannah was relieved to see Sandy's eyes light up and she came over and gave her a huge hug, too. She smelled of flowers and her body was soft against Savannah's.

"Mrs. Hodges dropped by earlier and showed me what a great job you did on her." Sandy beamed. "There's a job here for you any time you want it. How soon can you start?"

Her words were music to Savannah's ears, and she blushed as she looked over to the guys for approval.

"You'd better give it a day or two," Tom said. "She's just getting over a heavy cold. We'd hate to see her pass it on to all these good ladies."

"Carla suggested she might do some mobile work — you know, in the ladies' own homes, too?" Greg piped up.

"What a wonderful idea," Mrs. Taylor interjected. She was quite elderly and Savannah guessed that she wasn't always fit enough to make the journey to get her hair done. She'd heard her speaking to Mrs. Hodges when she'd dropped in for coffee and it seemed she wasn't in the best of health.

"That would be great. As you can see, we're a little short of space in here," Sandy chirped.

"Well, we can see you're busy. How about if Savannah comes to see you tomorrow to talk things over?" Tom put an arm around Savannah and she snuggled into him. She loved how the guys looked after her, and they were really in her corner here.

"Make it toward the end of the day. It's generally quieter then." Sandy nodded. "Who knows? We might even get time for a coffee."

"Thank you." Savannah beamed as they left.

"That went well, I thought," Greg said, once they were back on the sidewalk. "Hope we weren't too pushy, Savannah?"

"Not at all. Thanks so much."

"Looks like you've got yourself a job." Tom squeezed her.

"Now, all I need is somewhere to live," she said with a frown. In all the excitement, she hadn't thought that far ahead.

"Why not stay with us? We'll be coming into town every day, anyhow, so we can easily drive you to work and back. And you've seen how big the house is," Greg suggested.

She gawked at him. *This is a dream come true.*

Chapter Eleven

"Let's get over to the ranch then we can come back to the diner for some lunch while we make plans," Tom suggested, leading them back to where he'd parked the truck.

It only took a few minutes to get to the Shearer Ranch, which was just behind the main part of town. Fields spread out for miles and horses could be seen in the distance.

"The cattle we were talking about are in the field just beyond the house," Greg pointed out to Savannah, who seemed to be searching for them. "Come on. We'll show you."

They climbed out of the pickup and he held his arms out to help her down. He loved feeling her soft body next to his and pulled her in close.

"Looks like rain's on the way." Tom frowned at the darkening sky as they went toward a large field that lay on the east side of the ranch house.

Matt and Dyson were leaning over the fence, chatting with two other guys, who seemed vaguely familiar, even with their backs to them.

Greg and Tom each had an arm around Savannah's shoulders and Greg sensed her stiffen as they neared the other men. He wondered if she was just shy.

"You haven't met Matt yet, have you?" he said with a smile, indicating Dyson's identical twin as they arrived.

Matt held out a hand and she shook it. "Good to meet you, Savannah."

"You too," she murmured.

"Hey, boys, just can't keep away from the place, huh?" Dyson grinned. "Hi, Savannah. You feeling better?"

Her whole body tensed like a brick wall as she stared from him to the other two men, and Greg tightened his grip on her for fear she'd suddenly bolt like a skittish mare. He exchanged a concerned expression with Tom, who had clearly recognized the men at the same time he had.

"Guys, you remember Dan Edgerton and Pete Bramhall from Upton, don't you?" Matt introduced them politely, though his teeth were gritted as his jaw jutted out. "They just came over on spec to see if I'd made any decisions about their products yet."

"Yeah, we remember," Tom replied, curtly, and Greg noticed that he, too, had a strong grip on their girl. "What brings you all the way out here, guys? We didn't expect to see you again."

"Clearly." Dan and Pete were facing them now, both with faces as thunderous as the air around them. Dan scowled as he spoke, staring daggers at Savannah. "Well, well, this *is* a surprise."

"Why, Dan, you look like you've just seen a ghost," Tom sneered back, as Savannah appeared to shrink back into their arms.

Pete frowned. "Hey, I thought you said —"

"Yeah, we all did," Greg piped up, anger roiling in his stomach.

Dan was fuming and his chest puffed out like a robin in winter. "Savannah, what the hell are you doing here? I thought you were dead."

She wriggled in their arms but Greg held her even tighter. He knew she'd want to run away, but that wouldn't solve anything.

"You don't seem very pleased to find that she's not," he pointed out.

Dan frowned. "I...just...can't believe you're here." He continued to stare at her. "It's not every day you find the wife you thought you'd lost in the arms of a couple of other guys." His jaw was tight and his neck twitched.

"So...Savannah's your wife? Why would you think she was dead?" Dyson frowned.

Dan huffed. "She disappeared one night and never came back. I thought something awful must have happened to her." His steely gaze looked like it could cut Savannah in two.

"So, you reported her as missing?" Dyson clarified, though the look on his face showed that he already knew the answer.

"Yes."

"Well, that's funny, because there was nothing on file. I ran a check when I heard she was here, but there was nothing reported at all." Dyson straightened his back.

"Well, I mean...I was going to report it, but..."

"Go on." Dyson glared at him.

Dan huffed again, his lips tightening almost to nothing. "I was just hoping she was going to come back," he blurted.

Tom frowned. "So, why did you tell me she'd been killed on that railway crossing?"

Savannah gasped, staring up at Tom. She looked betrayed. *She was right to,* Greg thought.

Dan looked furious. What was more worrying was the way he was looking at Savannah—as though this was all her fault.

"I think it's time we were going," Pete said, his lips tight with anger. Greg figured that he didn't like being made a fool of, either.

"Not so fast," Dyson said holding a hand up to stop them. "First, I want to know exactly what's been going on here. And while you're at it, I want those details I was asking about Stone Supplements, too."

"We haven't got time," Dan said. He turned to go, but Tom quickly let go of Savannah and barred his way with his muscular frame.

"I could always arrest you first," Dyson said.

"On what grounds?" Pete Bramhall was clearly riled.

"Making false claims about those drugs you're peddling." Dyson looked very matter-of-fact.

"What drugs? We never said anything about drugs. Those supplements are purely herbal. They wouldn't have any effect on anything!"

"So, how else would they work?" Matt asked, frowning.

"They... They don't." Pete looked sheepish.

"So you're making false claims about them?" Dyson clarified. "Duly noted."

Dan glared at Pete. "You dumbass!"

"And you think that's worse than lying about your wife being dead?" Pete's hands went straight to his hips as he squared up to his business partner. "That's just sick, man!"

Big drops of rain started to fall as thunder rumbled overhead.

"Let's take this inside, shall we?" Dyson suggested.

Matt led the way, with the other two men following and Dyson bringing up the rear.

Tom slung his arm around Savannah, whose body was as stiff as a board. "Come on," he urged.

"I don't want to go in there," Savannah said, shaking her head. "I just want to go…"

"Home?" Greg offered. "You want to go back to Upton Crossing…with *him*?"

Her face was pale as she gaped up at him.

"It seems to me this is the only way we're going to find out what's going on," Tom said, as the rain became heavier. "Then, if you want to go back with him you can, or you can stay here with us. Either way, you'll get what's yours."

"And we'll get some answers," Greg added.

Savannah's body softened a little in their arms and she allowed them to lead her into the ranch house where the others were already sitting at a large dining table enjoying hot coffee and cookies. They hung their coats in the hall before venturing into the room.

"There you are." Matt smiled as they entered and he poured their drinks.

The atmosphere was tense as they took their seats, Greg being very careful to put Savannah between him and Tom and as far from Dan as they could.

"I think, as Savannah's here, that we should first discuss the matters that concern her," Dyson said, a pad of paper in front of him. "Then you can tell me all about this phony company you're working for."

Dan seethed.

Pete didn't look much happier.

"She just disappeared. What was I supposed to think?" Dan demanded, pointing at his wife.

Everyone turned to Savannah, who went bright red. At first, it looked as though she wasn't going to respond, and Greg put a comforting arm around her. She swallowed hard. "I was thrown out of the house. I wasn't even allowed to pack or get my coat." Tears welled in her eyes as she breathed deeply.

Greg held her a little tighter, his heart pummeling his ribs. He stared back at Dan, who was sneering at her.

"Liar. You just upped and left."

She shook her head. "I told you I wanted a divorce. You said if I didn't want you, I didn't get anything from the house. Then you opened the door and shouted at me to get out." Her voice was trembling.

Greg glanced over at Tom, who looked as sick as he felt. It all made sense, and he cursed himself for not being kinder to Savannah. He wished he'd spent more time with her, getting to know her. She was a beautiful woman and they had known something was wrong from the start. *Why the hell didn't I ask her more about herself?* He knew the answer. She was so cagey every time someone asked about her life that it was obvious she didn't want to discuss it. *That doesn't make it right, though.*

Savannah fought back tears as she stared at Daniel. She'd known he'd lie, but she had no idea he'd tell anyone that she'd *died*! And the guys knew. They'd met him and spoken to him. *Why didn't they tell me?*

"Well, I think you've already proven how well you can lie, Edgerton." Tom spoke through clenched teeth, glaring at Dan. "And it certainly explains why we found her on the back road in the middle of the night in a thunderstorm. For your information, she was soaked to the bone and hypothermic. Doc said it was a good thing we found her when we did."

Daniel stared at him. "You're lying!" He sounded vicious.

The table jolted as Tom moved to get up, but Dyson put his hand out to pacify him. "All right, Tom." He turned back to Daniel calmly. "Mr. Edgerton, why do you think we should believe *you* when you've already proven yourself to be mendacious?"

Savannah watched Daniel puff out his chest. He would hate that the sheriff used long words — something he would often do himself in order to make her feel stupid. It was good to see the tables turned for a change.

"I thought she was dead!" he hollered, thumping the table.

Savannah was glad of the distance between them. "More like you wished I was," she mumbled.

Daniel's face was bright red and his lips were practically invisible. His steely eyes bore into her and he leaned forward in his chair. "*You're* the one who's been gallivanting with other men!" he yelled. "Is *that* why you left me? To be with *them*?"

Savannah's jaw dropped and her heart thumped like a steam train. She shook her head. "No. It wasn't like that." Her voice was almost a whisper.

"Oh, that's right. Blame the lady. That's what bullies do, isn't it, Edgerton?" Greg sneered, holding her tighter.

Daniel shot to his feet, his chair flying backward. "What the hell have you been telling them?" he bawled at her. "I'll bet you claimed those bruises were down to me, too, didn't you? And that scar on your shoulder? I can just imagine you inventing lies about how they got there!"

Dyson and Matt stood and held onto Daniel firmly as he blurted out his accusations.

Savannah went hot all over. It had never occurred to her to tell anyone about his drunken attacks — not that she would expect anyone to believe her anyway. Daniel always seemed so controlled in company. No one would guess that he could hit the whiskey and turn violent.

She shook her head, realizing that he had all but confessed.

"You bastard!" Venom practically dripped from Greg's mouth as he derided her husband, and he stood, his fists clenched.

Savannah stared at him. Greg had always seemed so easy-going. She'd never imagined he could get this angry. Tom held her a little tighter as she gawked at all the men who were glaring at Daniel.

"Let's all just sit down," Dyson said, firmly.

Savannah's stomach roiled. "I'm gonna be sick," she muttered before bolting for the door.

The storm had eased and a heavy drizzle hung in the cold air. Savannah welcomed the chance to be alone with her thoughts, after churning her guts up all over Carla's daffodils.

She strolled over to a wooden bench that was placed against the front wall of the house and sat down, her legs trembling. Uncontrollable tears flooded her face and her whole body shivered. Everything had seemed so wonderful this morning—and now it was all ruined.

The miserable weather matched her thoughts as she sat with her head in hands. She was cold but it didn't matter—drenched, but she didn't care. Daniel had wrecked everything, just like he always did. She was glad that he was finally being exposed for the fraud that he was—but at what cost?

It didn't bother her that he'd lose his job and the house. She had no compassion for him now. The feelings that she'd had for those two cowboys had taught her that she had never loved Daniel—and she knew he could never have loved her. The fact that he wanted the world to think she was dead but wasn't prepared to grant her a divorce spoke volumes. He had always been a controlling bastard, though the outside world never saw that side of him.

What concerned her was that he had shown her up for the fool that she was. Everyone could see what she'd had to tolerate, living with Daniel, and they would think her stupid for putting up with it. He'd practically told them how he used to beat her. How would they feel about her now? And what about the fact that she'd lied about him being away and her having been out looking for a non-existent dog?

She became agitated and shot to her feet. The drive in front of her led to the track that joined the road into town. As she ran down it, as fast as she could with her barely-healed ankle, she could hear someone calling her back. But she didn't want to go back there. She'd get far away from here and start again someplace else, somewhere where they didn't know what a dumbass she was—a place where Daniel would never find her and ruin everything. That was what she thought she'd found at Pelican's Heath, but she'd been wrong. *Stupid...I didn't go far enough away. I should never have stopped here as long as I did. I certainly should never have started having feelings for...*

"Savannah!"

Tom gripped her with his strong hands, whirling her around as he stared at her. She almost slipped in the mud but he held her firmly.

"Get off me!" she yelled, as the rain continued to pour.

"No way. Where the hell are you going?"

"Away. That's all you need to know."

He frowned. "Why?"

"Maybe because I don't want to be around you anymore," she blurted out, conscious of the hurt look in those deep, dark eyes.

"What did I do?" He wasn't shouting anymore. He sounded sad, confused.

"You *knew*!" she hurled at him, trying to escape his grasp. "You'd met Daniel. You knew what he was saying about me – and yet you didn't tell me. You just let me make a damn fool of myself. Well, I hope you had a good laugh behind my back."

"It wasn't like that." Tom's voice was calm, which did nothing to pacify her.

"Oh no, of course it wasn't," she sneered. "I suppose you just bumped into him and didn't realize I was the wife he was claiming was dead? You didn't think anything about our names being the same or the fact he was from Upton Crossing, did you? It was all just a coincidence, I presume?"

He shook his head. "You've got it all wrong."

"Of course I have, because I'm so stupid. I'm bound to have misunderstood, aren't I?"

"Is that what he said? That you're *stupid*? That lying, conniving bastard back there said you were stupid, so you believed him? Is that it?"

She huffed, her mind whirring. "It doesn't matter. I just have to go."

"Then I'll take you. Where do you want to go?" He started to walk her back to the drive, but she pushed against him every step of the way.

"Leave me alone."

"Why? So you can run away?"

She stopped dead in her tracks, the rain falling heavier. She stared at him. His shirt was stuck to his body, outlining his muscles, and his dark hair dripped down his neck.

"What?"

"Well, that's just what you're doing, isn't it? It all got a bit tough in there, what with your husband turning up and showing us all how he's been treating you, admitting what he's done to you and lying his head off about a whole bunch of stuff. It wasn't easy for us to witness. I'm sure it was a lot harder for you. So, instead of standing up to him, you just run away. Despite the fact that the sheriff's got him dead to rights already. Setting aside that you know he can't touch you right now — or ever, once the sheriff locks him up."

He loosened his grip on her and held her more gently.

"Savannah, I get he's a bully and he threw you out the minute you told him you wanted a divorce. You had no choice but to get away from him then. But now you *have* a choice. You don't need to run away. He can't hurt you anymore. If you choose to stay, you can have a whole new life here at Pelican's Heath. You've already got a job lined up, a home — and two cowboys who are falling desperately in love with you." He moved a little closer to her, cloaking her in his musky scent. "It's your choice, Savannah. But we really want you to stay."

Her heart lurched as he took her in his arms and kissed her as though his life depended on it. He licked her lips, then he thrust his tongue into her mouth where he toyed with hers, sending tingles through her whole body. She closed her eyes as she got lost in another world, *his* world. A world of softness, of sensuality...of hope.

Chapter Twelve

"I don't know how, but you really seem to understand me." Savannah snuggled into his warmth as Tom led her back toward the house.

"Maybe we're more alike than you think," he said, pulling her a little closer. "I know how it feels to want to run away, but it never gets you anywhere. You still have the same problems, just in a different place. You have to learn to allow other people to do their jobs. They're trying to help you, so you need to let them."

"You really think Dyson will lock him up?" She frowned.

Tom nodded. "Looks that way to me. There's something real shady about that company they're working for, and the sheriff's determined to get to the bottom of it. He gets a real bee in his bonnet about people who deceive others for a quick buck. And now we know how that fuckwad treated you. Well, let's just say that he's even more bent on meting out justice."

Savannah could still taste Tom on her lips as they entered the house. They were both drenched and she shuddered, not sure if it was the cold or the way he made her feel that was sending quivers through her body. That kiss had solidified something between them, something she wasn't prepared to see broken by a bastard like Daniel Edgerton.

"Look at you two." Matt was on his feet in seconds, taking a couple of blankets from the hook behind the door to wrap around them.

The warmth was comforting, and Savannah pulled the red and white crocheted cover over her. Matt offered them both some milky hot chocolate and she looked over as Daniel gave a snort of derision.

"No prizes for guessing what you've been up to." He gave an ugly sneer.

"That's enough." Dyson sounded brutal, taking Savannah by surprise.

"Come and sit down," Greg urged.

"We really should get going. We need to get out of these wet things. Savannah's only just got over her illness. We can't risk her getting any worse." Tom frowned.

Greg stood as Daniel huffed.

"You don't know anything," Greg fired at him, pointing as he towered over the table. "Just keep your mouth shut where Savannah's concerned. She's had enough of your shit. She doesn't need any more." His mouth was tight as he spoke, and his restraint was palpable.

"Is that right?" Daniel stared at her.

"Yes, it is." Savannah jutted out her chin, taking a step toward him. "You treated me badly, Daniel. You threw me out like some piece of old trash when I pointed out that our marriage wasn't working. Then you pretended I was dead so you could get everyone's sympathy, instead of admitting what a bastard you'd been. But they'll know now. I'll make damn sure everyone at Upton Crossing knows what you've done. You're a cruel man, Daniel. An evil one. And I never want to see you again." Adrenalin pumped through her as she spoke, and her face grew hot, but she had to say it. For once in her life, she had to tell him exactly how it was.

"So you're going to leave me for one of these no-good cowboys. Is that it?" He gave the guys a disgusted look, waving his hand toward them in a flippant gesture.

"I'm not leaving you, Daniel. You threw me away, remember? So, what I choose to do with my life is none of your goddamn business." Fury raged through her as she raised her voice to him, pulling the blanket even tighter around her.

"Well said." Dyson was on his feet now. "Guys, if you want to take Savannah home, feel free. We've still got some unfinished business to discuss." He turned back to Daniel. "Give your wife the key to the matrimonial home. She'll need to fetch some belongings later."

Daniel's jaw fell open. "She's not getting into that house. It's mine."

"We'll let the judge decide that one," Dyson said. "In the meantime, give her the key so she can get some belongings."

The tic on Daniel's neck leaped into action as he glared at Savannah.

Dyson held out his hand. "Unless you want to add another charge to the list, I suggest you give me that key right now." His voice was more of a growl, as he dared the man to defy him.

Reluctantly, Daniel put his hand into his pocket and slammed the key onto the table. It was attached to a key ring in the shape of a large silver D.

Dyson rolled his eyes but picked it up and gave it to Savannah. "You've got all night. He won't be going farther than the cell," he assured her.

Relief washed over her. At last, she was going to be free of Daniel for good.

"Come on." Greg ushered her and Tom out of the house, pulling on their coats as they went back out into the storm, which had intensified again. "I'll drive."

She climbed in between them and thunder rolled as he turned the engine. "We'll go back to our place," Greg said. "You can get into something dry, then we'll go over and get your stuff. We can stop on the way for something to eat."

Savannah watched his gorgeous face as he drove them back through Pelican's Heath and toward Bracken Ridge. He was cool and confident. She found it comforting that he had everything planned out. It was what she needed. *He* was what she needed.

She closed her eyes and snuggled into the warmth of the two guys, breathing in their fragrances. They were both so different and yet she couldn't choose between them, not that she'd want to. Together, they were the full package, everything she could ever want.

As they pulled up outside the house, she had an unexpected feeling of belonging, of being home. She had never felt that way at Upton Crossing. Daniel had chosen the house and everything in it. He'd said it was his job, as man of the house. In fact, he had been just controlling their environment in the same way he'd controlled her.

"Come on. Let's get you out of those wet things," Tom said, holding his arms out to help her down.

"You can talk. Look at the state of you," she pointed out with a grin. He was soaked to the skin under that coat, as was she, and he trembled as he lifted her from the truck.

Greg unlocked the door and they all piled in, grateful to slam the door against the relentless rain. Savannah followed Tom upstairs while Greg went toward the kitchen.

"This is the spare room," Tom said, opening the door of a large bedroom. It didn't echo like the rest of the house, having been furnished with a huge bed that dominated the room, and wardrobes lining three of the walls.

"Wow." It was tastefully decorated in cream and pale blue, with floor-to-ceiling drapes in dark blue velour.

"Like it? We still have the rest of the house to do, but thought the bedrooms were the most important rooms to start with." Tom unzipped one of the bags they'd brought from the guest house and threw a towel to her. "Our rooms are just down the hall. The shower's through there." He pointed. "Have it as hot as you need."

Savannah went over to the en-suite bathroom, which afforded a corner bath as well as a huge walk-in shower. She wasted no time in peeling off her sodden clothes, which she left in a heap on the floor in her haste to get under the stream of warm water. Her whole body sagged as she relaxed into the heat, and she closed her eyes to savor the sensations.

"Need any help in there?" Tom's soft baritone seeped into her mind and she opened her eyes in shock.

"What?" She peeped around the shower screen and her jaw dropped.

Tom was casually leaning against the doorframe. Not only was he smiling, he was also naked. Despite her best intentions, her gaze was drawn to his ripped chest with its smattering of dark hair, his tight six-pack and — *oh good Lord* — his cock. It was even bigger than she'd imagined — or hoped — and she gasped at the sight.

His body shuddered, reminding her that he had also been caught out in the cold rain, and she frowned.

"I could wash your back, if you'd like?" he offered, his dark eyes glinting with promise.

Savannah gaped at him. She'd never had an offer like that before. And she'd never seen a guy like him before. He seemed relaxed, smiling at her while her mind raced. Every fiber in her being was willing her to accept his offer, but something — or, rather, some*one* — held her back.

"I'm a married woman," she mumbled miserably.

He pursed his lips. "And you don't want to be accused of adultery?"

She sighed. "Does that make me even more stupid?"

He shook his head. "No. But it doesn't mean I can't wash your back." His lips twitched and his eyes twinkled in question.

"Just…wash my back?"

"Yup. If that's what you want?"

She nodded slowly, belying the excitement that fluttered in her stomach.

Watching him slink across the room toward her reminded Savannah of a cat rounding on a tiny mouse.

His taut body was soon behind her in the warm shower and he stretched his strong arm effortlessly around her to take a sponge and tube of shower gel from the shelf to her left.

He smothered her in his fragrance, caressing her back with the sponge, then his fingers. Her nerves dissipated and she sighed, placing her palms flat against the tiled wall in front of her to steady herself as she melted into his caress.

"Did anyone ever tell you what a beautiful body you have?" His voice was as silky smooth as the gel on her back, and his breath was warm against her cheek.

A mixture of elation and embarrassment ran through her. She shook her head, momentarily unable to speak.

"Then you haven't been with the right people," he replied.

His nonchalant reply took her by surprise and she giggled. "Like who?"

"Me, for instance." She felt him shrug behind her and smiled.

"And me."

Savannah froze as she heard Greg's voice echo around the bathroom.

"You took your time," Tom said, massaging her back.

"I put the coffee pot on. Any more of that cocoa and you'd both be asleep," Greg replied. "Then we'd never get over to Upton Crossing."

Savannah swallowed hard at the thought of going back there. Her euphoria dissipated quicker than water down a plughole and she tensed, turning her head to one side. She still hadn't looked over at Greg, afraid that he'd be jealous that she was in the shower with Tom, part of her afraid he'd also be naked—and with both of them, she'd be powerless to resist.

"You're right. We should go now," she said. "Could you please hand me a towel?" She reached out her hand, and only then did she face Greg.

"Are you sure? I didn't mean…" He was frowning in confusion as he stood in the middle of the room in nothing but his Levi's.

She gulped. He looked gorgeous. His torso was ripped, like Tom's, but it looked as smooth as satin. His muscles rippled as he leaned over and took a towel from the rack beside him, holding it out to her.

"Quite sure. Thanks." She nodded, taking the towel from him.

"We don't need to go yet," Tom objected, but she was already stepping out of the cubicle, swathed in the huge bath sheet.

Greg took her arm. "I didn't mean to go right away."

"No, but you're right. We should get some coffee and hit the road. If this storm continues, some of the roads will be swamped. It'd be better to get there in daylight." Her voice was a little more clipped than she'd intended, as she tried to take the sensible approach, though it was the last thing she really wanted to do.

"You can borrow some dry clothes." Greg sounded resigned as he led her through to the bedroom.

"Thank you. It'll be good to get my clothes back — especially some more underwear." She smiled as he handed her a pair of jeans and a sweater.

"Underwear?" Tom looked mortified as he followed them through.

Savannah rolled her eyes. "I'll change through there," she said, gesturing the bathroom.

"There's no need…" Greg began.

"It's fine." She marched back into the steamy en suite and closed the door with a sigh.

Drying herself briskly, she recalled the feel of Tom's large hands on her back. He was so gentle with her that she hadn't wanted it to end, especially not with thoughts of going back to Upton Crossing.

She wiped the mirror and stared at her reflection. She'd wanted Tom. And she could tell he wanted her, too, though he respected her wishes. She wondered how long her resolve would have lasted, though, had they been left to their own devices. Greg had looked stunning in just his jeans, and she wondered if he would have joined them in the shower. Her heart hammered at the thought.

She stared at the look of longing on her own face. She had never looked — or felt — anything like this before. Her cheeks were flushed, though it was a warm room, she told herself. Her eyes looked larger than usual and her lips were almost dark red.

Raised voices made her jump and she looked toward the door.

"What the hell did you do that for? You ruined everything!" Tom was clearly annoyed.

"You were the one who asked what had kept me. I was only answering your question. How was I to know she'd want to leave right away?"

"You practically said we needed to hurry."

"I did not."

"You implied it."

"No, I didn't."

The argument continued as she quickly pulled on the clothes then flung open the door. They both stared at her, silenced by shock.

"Let's just get this over with, shall we?" Her lips were tight as she spoke.

Greg pulled on his boots, his face tense.

"I'm getting a coffee." Tom, now dressed, turned and left the room.

"Here." Greg handed her a comb that she pulled through her damp hair. "And you can borrow these." He passed her a pair of Tom's boots.

Had she not been so disappointed, she would have sniggered at the thought of him lending her Tom's belongings. It made sense, as Tom's feet were a size smaller than his own, but it would still have been prudent to ask Tom's permission.

"Thanks."

"Look. I didn't mean to spoil your fun," he said, rubbing his hands together.

"It's fine."

"No, it's not. You're both pissed with me."

"We're not."

"You are, and I can see why. But I didn't mean we had to leave right away. I'd have loved to stay and have some fun before we left."

Savannah gaped at him, imagining what kind of fun he would have loved to have with them — the sort *she* would also have enjoyed. "We need to get going," she said on a sigh.

He took a step close to her, holding her arm. "Are you sure you're okay? With everything that's happened, I mean?"

She nodded. "I'm fine."

She was about to move but he stopped her, tightening his grip on her arm. "You don't look it."

Gazing up at him in surprise, she noticed how he was studying her face. "What's that supposed to mean?"

"It means I know you're pissed with me. Why don't you just come right out and admit it? Tell the truth."

His voice was a little raised and she glared at him, annoyed at his tone.

"The truth." She bit her lip as she tried to curb her rising temper. "The truth about what, Greg? You think I've been lying to you, is that it?" She wrenched her arm from his grip.

"That's not what I said."

"But it's what you implied." Her voice rose a little now. "I told you where I was from. I told you my name and that I was married. What part of that was a lie?"

"None of it except the excuse about the dog."

"And yet, you and Tom neglected to tell me that you'd met my husband. You practically brought him here with your so-called business negotiations, which I tried to steer you away from, if you recall?"

"Yes, I do. But we didn't realize that was who Matt was going to meet up with over at Upton."

"But you knew exactly who he was when you met him?"

"Yes, ma'am."

"And yet you didn't tell me? Isn't an omission of the truth the same as lying?"

Greg sighed. "It wasn't meant to be."

"But it was."

He huffed. "We were trying to protect you. When we realized who we were dealing with, we wanted to find out why he was lying about you. We couldn't just come right out and tell you we'd met your husband, but he was going around telling everyone that you were dead, now could we? That would be cruel."

"Unlike lying to me?"

"We wanted to find out what the hell his game was, why he was saying those things about you. It was clear there was something wrong if he was saying you were dead, and yet you obviously thought you couldn't be with us because you were married to him. It just didn't add up."

"I never said that." She gaped at him, her heart thumping.

"No, but you implied it."

"He's got a point there, darlin'." Tom stood in the doorway, a large cup of coffee in one hand.

She looked from one gorgeous, righteous-looking face to the other, feeling like an animal caught in a snare. Her mouth dropped open but no words fell out. Her mind whizzed as she tried to think of a snarky reply—or a true reply. Or any reply, just to cut into the deafening silence that cloaked them. "We should go," she snapped at last.

Tom sniggered. "I think that's what you call a stalemate."

Greg grinned, though Savannah chose to ignore it as she stalked past Tom and down the stairs.

"I made up a thermos bottle and grabbed a couple of blankets, just in case," Tom said when they reached the kitchen. He lifted a box from the counter. Greg took their coats from where they'd hung them on a hook behind the door, and they all headed out.

"At least the rain's stopped," Greg remarked as he followed Savannah around to the passenger side of the truck.

"Yeah, but it's already starting to get dark." Tom frowned at the dull sky.

Savannah refused Greg's hand as he offered to help her into her seat and sat as upright as she could, so as not to touch either of them once they were all in position.

Tom drove this time and she watched him maneuver the pickup off the driveway and out onto the road. His scent wafted over her and she couldn't be sure whether it had come from him or from herself, now that they had shared the same shower gel. The thought returned her to the feeling of his hands on her back and she sank into the seat with a sigh.

With a grin, Tom looked over at her, and she wondered, not for the first time, if he had read her mind. In a way she hoped he had, that he was capable of such a thing. That would save him asking the questions she knew he'd been burning to ask since he saw her naked body. Was Daniel responsible for the scar on her shoulder? And why was it such a weird shape?

Chapter Thirteen

The roads were passable for the truck, and they even chanced a stop at a fast food restaurant for some burgers and fries on the way. The atmosphere between them lifted a little, although Savannah slept for some of the journey. The rain held off and they made it to the railway at Upton Crossing just after nightfall.

"There's the house." Savannah pointed to a cottage that stood alone at the side of the track.

Tom frowned. "Does he always leave a light on?"

She felt indignant as they pulled up outside and noticed that not only was the outside light on, but one of the downstairs ones was, too. "He always complained about the bills," she told them. "I had to use a candle if I wanted to read at night because he thought it was a waste of electricity having the lamp on for just one of us, even when he was out at the bar."

"He didn't mind spending money on beer, then?" Greg shook his head and they clambered out of the truck.

"He's planted flowers," she remarked as they walked up the garden path to the front door. "It didn't look this nice when I left."

Tom slung an arm around her, sensing her disappointment. She took out the key and put it in the lock. The door opened easily.

"He didn't lock up." Her voice was a horrified whisper.

"I'll go first." Greg barged past her before she could object and stepped into the tiny hallway.

Seconds later, there was a high-pitched scream.

Savannah and Tom rushed in after him.

"She's got a knife," Greg yelled before they reached him. He had his palms face up and was standing in the doorway of the kitchen.

"Who?" Savannah demanded, almost screaming herself.

"My name's Greg Jackson. Who are you?" Greg's voice was calm as he spoke to the female.

"That's none of your business. You're trespassing, and I'm calling the sheriff," came the reply.

Savannah seethed. It sounded like a young woman. *In my house!*

"Good. Dyson Shearer was the one who gave us the key and told us to get down here," he replied.

"Gave you a key?" She sounded incredulous.

"Well, gave it to Savannah, really." He held out his hand and Savannah took a couple of steps closer and passed it to him. He held it up for the woman to see.

"That's Daniel's key!" she hollered. "Where did you get it? Where is he? If you've done something to him, I'll—"

"Never mind waving that knife at me," Greg said, shaking his head. "What are you doing in this house? And how do you know Daniel?"

"I *live* here!" she shouted, "not that it's any of your damn business. Now, what the hell have you done with my fiancé?"

Savannah's whole body grew hot and she barged past Greg to see the woman for herself.

"Your *what*?" she demanded, furious at the sight of another woman in her kitchen.

"Who the hell are you?" the woman yelled, taking a step closer to the doorway, pointing the knife at her.

"I'm Savannah Edgerton. Daniel's *wife*."

"You can't be!"

"Well, I am, so get used to it. And while we're on the subject, who the hell are you and what're you doing in my house?" Savannah hollered.

"But you died. He told me. He told everyone that his wife died. He's a widower." She looked stunned.

"As you can see, I'm not dead — and Daniel's a liar." Savannah didn't know whether to hate the woman or pity her. One thing was for sure, though. She didn't like her.

"Where is he?" The woman looked unnerved but was still the one holding the knife.

"He's in a police cell," Greg told her. "Call Sheriff Shearer. He'll tell you."

"Which is where *you* should be for trespassing in my house," Savannah snapped, sickened that this woman seemed to think she had the upper hand while she'd been having an affair with Daniel.

"This is *my* house now," she replied.

"Well you wasted no time in elbowing your way in. I've only been gone a couple of weeks," Savannah pointed out.

"No, he told me he's been a widower for months. I wouldn't have been going out with him otherwise." The cloud of realization covered the woman's face as she spoke, and Savannah bit her tongue while the truth sunk in for all of them.

"How long have you been seeing Daniel?" Greg stepped into the kitchen, brushing past Savannah as he went right up to the woman and snatched the knife from her hand.

The woman looked like she was in a daze as she stared up at him.

"I'm Belinda Hathaway. I've worked with Daniel for three years," she said. "We've always been close. He used to flirt with me, but I didn't take him seriously. We'd been out for the odd drink, maybe a meal or two, but that was it. He was married. I told him I'd never fool around with a married man. Then, one night a couple of weeks ago, he brought me home. Here. He told me that Savannah had passed away a couple of months back, but he hadn't told anyone at work so they wouldn't pity him. He said he couldn't stand the thought of all those sorrowful looks."

"And you believed him?" Greg asked.

Tom closed the front door and followed them into the kitchen.

"Of course." She shrugged.

"So, you slept with him? In my bed? That first night when he brought you back here and told you I was dead?" Savannah asked.

"Well…yes. I'd believed him. Why wouldn't I?"

"Because it wasn't true!" Savannah yelled at her.

"How the hell was I supposed to know?"

"Oh, yeah, because he's so reliable," Savannah sneered.

"Well, I didn't know he was lying, did I?"

"This is ludicrous!" Savannah shouted. "I'll just take my things and get out of here. You can sort it out with Daniel when he gets back."

"You're not taking anything from this house," Belinda screeched. "If Daniel isn't here to approve it, you'll take nothing."

"You're right. This is stupid." Tom pulled out his cell phone and called the sheriff. "Dyson. We're at the Edgerton's house. There's a woman here called Belinda Hathaway who has moved in with Daniel. Did you know about this?"

Dyson's expletives could be heard on the phone just before Tom hung up.

"He'll call me back in a minute," he explained.

"Good. In the meantime, I'll get my stuff." Savannah was adamant, but Belinda grabbed her by the hair and screamed at her.

"Oh, no, you won't!"

"Get the fuck off me!" Savannah was outraged — and sore.

"Stop that!" Tom's voice was deep and loud, stunning the women into silence.

Belinda let go of Savannah's hair and took a step back.

"Why don't you just calm down and we'll see what the sheriff's got to say?" Tom's voice was a little quieter now but no less dominant.

"I shouldn't have to. This is my house and I just want my clothes. He can have the rest." Savannah knew she sounded like a sulky schoolgirl, but that didn't matter right now.

Tom's cell rang, and he answered straight away. "Hi, Sheriff." He glanced at Belinda before turning his back on them and going back into the hall to finish the conversation.

"How were you planning to marry Daniel while he was still married to me?" Savannah glowered at Belinda.

"I told you. He said you were dead," Belinda snapped.

"And you didn't bother to check if he had a death certificate?"

"Why would I?"

"Well, you'd need it for the registrar," Savannah sneered, suddenly feeling a sense of one-upmanship. Daniel wouldn't allow her a divorce, but he wouldn't be able to remarry without one. *It sure looks like the fucker shot himself in the foot there.*

Belinda stared back at her, a look of realization misting her eyes.

"It seems you weren't the only one to be taken in by him," Greg said, walking over to Savannah.

"Well, it's a good thing the sheriff's got him behind bars," Tom stated, walking back into the room. "Dyson just asked him about Belinda and Daniel's gone mad. I could hear him yelling in the background. He's claiming that Belinda's just a friend and must have popped over to do some cleaning or something."

Belinda's face crumpled as huge tears flooded her cheeks. "How could h-he?" She sobbed. "We were going to get married, have kids…everything."

Savannah felt a pang in her heart. The thought of Daniel wanting to start a family with Belinda hurt more than anything, but she still couldn't bear to see anyone crying. She put an arm around her. "Maybe you still will," she offered. "I'll be out of here for good once I've got my things. You're welcome to Daniel—and the sooner he agrees to a divorce, the better."

Belinda tensed in her arms and lifted her head with a sniff. "You don't honestly think I'd want him after this, do you? He's lied his head off and made a fool of me. I want nothing more to do with him. I'll be taking my things and moving out of here tonight, too, so you just take whatever you want. Though I'll warn you, besides a small trunk in the bedroom, I haven't seen any of your clothes. Daniel must have gotten rid of them."

"Sheriff said to take whatever's yours," Tom told Savannah.

Belinda pulled out of her arms and marched through to the living room, brushing past Tom on her way.

"You want anything besides your clothes?" Greg asked.

Savannah shook her head. "I'll just see what he's kept in that trunk."

She went straight into the bedroom. Everything was as she'd left it. The photograph on the wall, the knickknacks on the little shelf. Memories flooded back to her, and for a moment, she thought she was back in that world with Daniel. She became edgy, nervous, as though Daniel would walk into the room at any minute, reeking of beer and demanding sex. She shuddered.

"Are you okay?" Tom appeared in the doorway, pulling her from her miserable thoughts.

She looked over at him. He hadn't even entered the room. He frowned with concern and oozed sympathy and care—and he was gorgeous. A vision of his naked body in the bathroom earlier flashed through her mind, accompanied by the feelings he had invoked in her—

longing, excitement, hope. She had never experienced any of those with Daniel, and yet, like a fool, she had allowed him to hold her back from taking things further with Tom, from following her instincts and desires.

Gazing around the room, Savannah saw nothing but misery and heartache. Every piece of furniture held recollections of the sadness she had endured while staring at it, and every ornament carried a remembrance she would rather forget.

"I don't want anything," she said.

Tom nodded. He understood. Somehow, she just knew he would. "We'll go as soon as you're ready, beautiful."

She sniffed back a tear as a lump caught in her throat. "Now," she whispered.

The journey back to Bracken Ridge was quiet. Savannah snuggled up close to Greg, who had an arm around her, while Tom reached over to stroke her arm while he drove. She remembered crying but must have fallen asleep after a while as the next thing she knew Greg was carrying her into their house.

"I can walk," she told him with a grateful smile. Her voice echoed in the emptiness.

"I didn't want you sleepwalking," he teased, putting her down in the hallway. "You could have ended up in a ditch."

She rolled her eyes, recalling the night they had found her. She often wondered why she hadn't been nicer to them on that first meeting. Again, it had been Daniel's influence that had made her so guarded, she guessed.

"There's not much to eat, unless you like chips," Tom said with a grimace, following them in. "That café won't be open at this time of night, though I can always take a drive into town and see if I can pick up some food? Or we could go back to the guest house. Mrs. H always has something to eat."

"I'm really not hungry," Savannah said. "I kind of lost my appetite back at the house." She didn't want to go back tonight and have to tell Mrs. Hodges all about their day while it was all so raw.

"I can understand that." Greg put a comforting arm around her. "It must've been hard."

She relished his warmth.

Tom stretched. "Well, we can always take a couple of bags of potato chips and head up to bed. If we all use the spare room, there's a TV up there we can watch, if no one's tired," he suggested, raising his eyebrows

"That sounds like fun." Savannah was a little nervous about staying with them all night, but she was also excited.

"Good idea, buddy," Greg said, with a nod. "We'll see you up there." He led Savannah up the stairs while Tom disappeared toward the kitchen.

"I can't get over how big this is," she marveled as he followed her into the spare bedroom.

"It seemed even bigger before we got the furniture in," Greg said, looking around the room.

"It's almost the size of my whole house." The thought brought back visions of Upton Crossing and she cursed herself for ruining her own fun.

"You'll have to suffer Tom's snoring, I'm afraid," Greg said with a wink as he handed her a T-shirt to wear. "I keep meaning to get more earplugs. I'll get you some, too, if you'd like. It's been a nightmare having to share a room at the B-and-B." He grinned at her and she managed a smile back.

"I do *not* snore," Tom retorted as he entered the room with his arms full of bags of potato chips. "For your information, I have never snored in my life."

"Well, not while he was awake, anyway," Greg joked, removing his shirt.

Tom shook his head. "Don't listen to him, beautiful," he urged.

Savannah giggled, relieved at how relaxed they all were in the bedroom. With Daniel, there had been no fun, no joking and every insult he had thrown at her had been for real. She was glad to think that she wouldn't ever have to go back there again.

"Can I just use the bathroom?" she asked, licking her lips at the sight of Greg's naked torso.

"Of course. And you don't need to ask. Just think of this place as your home." Greg smiled.

Her stomach lurched. She would love this to be her home...with them. "Thanks."

She dived into the en suite, panting as she leaned against the door. She splashed cold water on her face and undressed.

"You'll have to hurry if you don't want Greg to eat all the potato chips," Tom called to her after a few minutes.

Savannah took a deep breath and emerged from the bathroom, wearing the large T-shirt and a nervous smile. She'd combed her hair, which now lay in flaming swathes around her shoulders, and her face was heated with anticipation.

Greg was already in bed eating chips, and candles flickered on the nightstands at each side of the bed. He sat up straight, smiling when he saw her.

Tom was standing at the end of the bed in his shorts. His excitement also showed. He winked at her, making her flush even more. "You're so beautiful," he murmured.

"Get in here. The film's about to start," Greg urged, pulling back the covers.

Savannah clambered into the bed, which was wide enough for three pillows along the headboard and longer than a California king-size. She guessed the guys had had all the beds custom-made for their needs, and it was very comfortable.

Tom jumped in beside her, placing the TV remote on the nightstand and, despite all the extra room, both guys scooted over and cuddled into her.

Their bodies were hard against hers, but their voices were soft. Savannah lay on her side with her head on Greg's chest and his arm around her. Tom snuggled into her back, his arm around her waist.

"Are you okay, sweetheart?" Greg murmured.

"Yeah." She nodded and smiled. She couldn't recall a time when she had been more okay.

"Hope you're not getting chips in the bed," Tom grumbled as the film sprang into action.

Greg snorted, feeding a few to Savannah, while they lay watching the huge TV on the wall opposite them.

She relished Greg stroking her shoulder, while Tom caressed her stomach through the T-shirt that she now regretted wearing.

Chapter Fourteen

Judging by the soft music playing in the background, Savannah guessed the guys had put on a romantic movie, but she wasn't paying any attention. Instead, she was more interested in the attention both guys were lavishing on her.

Beneath her ear, Greg's heartbeat had picked up the pace, and Tom's cock hardened even more against her thigh. It had been evident through his shorts, ever since she'd joined them in bed. Despite the effect she was having on them, which surprised and delighted her, the atmosphere was much lighter and easier than she had expected.

Greg teased her with a potato chip, putting it to her lips then pulling it away again. She giggled. He was such fun, while at the same time, his eyes glinted with promise.

Tom didn't appear uncomfortable at all, in spite of his thickening erection, and he nuzzled her neck. His breath was hot against her skin, and she moaned at the sensation of his stubble grazing her flesh. His words from earlier rang in her ears, *'two cowboys who are desperately falling in love with you,'* melting her heart and filling her with hope.

After Daniel's revelations, she no longer held any guilt about being with the gorgeous guys and regretted that it had taken her so long to admit to herself that what she felt for them was a million times more than she could ever feel for him. She closed her eyes to stop herself from analyzing the situation and tried to clear her mind, allowing the guys' ministrations to intensify and overtake her thoughts.

"You really are gorgeous," Tom whispered in her ear before nibbling at her lobe.

Savannah had never been called that before and her face heated. The sensations of his mouth on her ear caused her whole body to glow as he proceeded to lick and suck the area, which, she realized, was much more erogenous than she had ever expected.

Her stomach burned and her pussy became wet as electricity seemed to zing through her whole body. She moaned, swinging one leg in between Greg's to allow her some purchase against her aching clit.

Tom draped his hand down to her thigh that straddled Greg's leg. His caresses were soft but urgent and his breathing became heavier as he continued to torment her ear and nip at her neck.

Greg's cock had stiffened against her leg and he bent his head down to take her lips in a lingering kiss. His tongue was soft but determined as he licked at her seam then pushed it into her mouth, exploring and owning every inch of it with the surety of a man who knew what he wanted.

The confident ministrations of the two men caused a gush to escape her pussy and she pressed it hard against Greg's leg, her inhibitions crumbling like sand on a hot day. Spurred on by her actions, Tom ran his hand up her thigh and caressed her butt, which was no longer covered by the T-shirt.

She hummed against Greg's tongue and almost bit down hard when Tom slipped his fingers between her ass cheeks. Yelping into Greg's mouth, she sensed a tingle in her perineum and clenched hard as his thumb traveled upward.

"I'm guessing you've never had it here?" Tom murmured into her ear. He pressed gently against her tight opening.

Again her face grew hot, and she shook her head. Greg sniggered, still toying with her tongue, and she heard Tom's chuckle from deep within his throat. Both guys were so close to her now as they writhed against her. Tom's covered erection aligned with her back entrance, touching nerves she never knew she had. Greg's huge cock grazed dangerously against her hand, which lay on his stomach. Her right arm was wedged between her body and Greg's side, though she could feel his flushed skin against hers, and she stroked his muscular hip through his shorts.

She rubbed against Greg's leg as the need grew in her pussy, and she fought to position her clit against his flesh for purchase. Tom's cock followed her, still aligned between her ass cheeks, inducing unbelievable sensations that racked her whole body. Her nipples were hard and she was sure Greg could feel them against his skin, even through the T-shirt.

Greg stroked her leg that lay over his, skimming her flesh with his short nails and causing her to clench and unclench her body in anticipation.

"I want you," Tom whispered, as he licked the shell of her ear.

Her breath hitched.

"What he said," Greg murmured once he freed her mouth.

There was nothing she wanted more, and she groaned her assent while Tom stroked her as he pulled the T-shirt over her head. She sat up, still straddling Greg's thigh. Relief swept through her as the cooler air kissed her skin, and she was glad the room was in semi-darkness, with just the flickering of the candles and the TV casting shadows around them.

Tom hopped off the bed to remove his shorts, reminding Savannah that she needed to move so Greg could do the same. She flushed at the amount of fluid trickling down his thigh once she lifted her leg from his, but his nonchalant smile told her there was nothing to worry about.

The mattress dipped behind her as Tom returned to the bed, and he began to massage her shoulders while she sat with her back to him.

"Ooh, that's lovely," she moaned, relaxing again.

He was close enough for her to feel the heat from his body and to smell his musky scent, and she leaned her head back against him while he worked his magic on her muscles.

"Let me taste you," Greg murmured, kneeling on the bed as he edged toward her, his massive cock standing at attention.

Savannah's stomach burned again and she sat bolt upright. Daniel had never done that, and she had often wondered what it would feel like.

The twinkle had returned to Greg's eyes and his lips were upturned. "Only if you want me to," he added.

She swallowed hard. *How could I refuse?*

"Is that a yes?" Greg had moved no closer since asking, and she sensed that neither of the guys would dream of doing anything she didn't want.

She nodded with a smile.

Tom fluffed the pillows and she lay back, her heart pummeling her ribs. From this position, she could see both guys silhouetted against the TV screen, their cocks thick and hard, though in no way threatening or intimidating. She guessed it was the self-control that the guys demonstrated that took the fear out of the situation. Daniel had usually been drunk by the time he came to bed and there had been no way she could refuse him anything without suffering the consequences.

"Do you want to taste me?" Tom asked her, and she stared at his handsome face, his eyes shining in the candle light.

"Um, I've never..." she murmured, hoping she wouldn't disappoint him but longing to try it.

He smiled. "That's okay. You don't have to—"

"No, it's not that," she said quickly. "It's just..."

He looked at her questioningly, waiting for her to clarify.

She took a deep breath, looking from one gorgeous face to the other.

"I want to try...everything." She jutted her chin out. "I know I haven't done much before, but I want to, with you." Again she looked at them both in turn, hoping her eyes would reiterate her words.

"All right, but if you want us to stop, you just have to say the word, ya hear?" Greg said, smiling.

"I will," she promised.

It was all the confirmation they needed, as both guys got into position, Greg pulling her legs gently apart and inhaling her fragrance, while Tom straddled her shoulders.

"Great, I guess this means I get your butt in my face," Greg moaned as Tom got comfortable.

"Hey, don't knock it. Not everyone gets that much pleasure in their life." Tom grinned over his shoulder.

Savannah giggled. She loved their banter, which always eased the atmosphere. "Hello again," she said as Tom held his cock just a little distance from her mouth.

"Hmm, you're getting to see quite a lot of him today, ain't ya?" Tom said with a smile.

"Hey, guys. I'm getting a little jealous back here," Greg piped up.

"I'm sure your time'll come, bro," Tom assured him, winking at Savannah, who nodded.

"That's not all that's gonna come," Greg murmured.

"Promises, promises..." Savannah said, rolling her eyes with a giggle. Their sense of humor seemed to embolden her.

Tom chuckled.

"Oh, yeah. And I *always* keep my promises," Greg replied in a deep, soft voice that sent tingles through Savannah.

In the next second, Greg swiped her pussy with his tongue and she yelped in surprise and delight.

Tom chuckled, placing his weeping cock on her lip, where she lapped at his juices. He tasted sweeter than she'd expected and not at all unpleasant.

Greg licked her pussy, sucking her labia and tugging at the sensitive flesh inside. "You're so wonderful, sweetheart," he murmured.

He used his fingers to hold her open, stroking her all around her clit, but not quite touching it this time. She moaned at the sensations as pleasure swept through her whole body.

She reached up and stroked the soft hairs of Tom's chest while licking all around his bulbous cockhead. She dipped her tongue into its eye and swiped it down the slit, eliciting a sharp hissing sound.

"Oh yeah, beautiful," he groaned, arching his back. As his chest puffed out, she rubbed his nipples between her thumbs and forefingers, rolling gently.

To her delight, Tom hummed. Empowered by his reaction, she took more of his cock into her mouth, relaxing her throat to allow for its length. Its girth touched the insides of her cheeks and she tipped her head up to feel its tip on the soft skin of her gullet. Sucking hard, she relished Tom's groans of excitement and joined in with moans of her own as Greg kissed lightly on her sensitive areas.

The air was filled with murmurs and whispers, hisses and gasps — and the heavy scent of sex.

Savannah became more heated and sucked hard on Tom's cock as Greg teased her clit with his tongue. When she thought she could take no more, Greg swiped right over her throbbing nub and she screamed as the cock in her mouth swelled even more.

"I'm gonna come!" Tom's panicked cry surprised her as he tried to pull out of her mouth.

She grabbed his cock, staring up at him with pleading eyes. His juices had already begun trickling down her throat and she relished the taste. She wanted more.

He looked stunned. "Are you sure?"

She nodded emphatically, trying to keep her mouth closed around him her throat was filled by his thick cum. She arched her back, offering her pussy up to Greg, willing him not to stop licking and sucking. He pushed his fingers into her tight hole and her muscles gripped them, never wanting to let go.

Tom roared his release and a surge of cum shot down her throat agaom, filling her mouth.

"Oh God!" Tom hollered.

Savannah screwed her eyes shut as an almighty wave of pleasure coursed through her, and she gripped Tom's cock hard in one hand while grasping at his muscular arm with the other. Greg swiped her nub over and over as she rode out her crescendo.

She became aware that Tom's cock had shrunk and he withdrew from her mouth while she licked the last of the delicious cream from its shaft. She opened her eyes to see sweat pouring from his face while he beamed down at her, panting hard. He lifted himself to one side of her, rubbing his knees, which must have been in agony as he had kept his weight on them the whole time.

Greg licked the last of her juices from her pussy while Tom hobbled to the bathroom.

"Are you okay, sweetheart?" Greg asked with a grin. His finger still swirled around her folds, keeping her on edge.

He seemed to be the only one capable of talking right then, although she noticed even his voice was husky. She nodded, smiling back at him.

Tom returned and offered her a glass of water from the bathroom. "I thought you could use this." He winked. She sat up and took it, relishing its coldness. When she'd had her fill, he took it from her, placed it on the nightstand, leaned in and took her in his arms for a lingering kiss that tingled right down to her already-awakened groin.

Greg chuckled and she guessed he'd felt her clench with excitement, as his fingers were still teasing her sensitized areas. She didn't mind. Tom's kiss was tender and lasting, and she didn't want it to stop.

"I wanna make love to you, sweetheart." Greg's deep murmur permeated the euphoric mush in her brain and she slowly computed his words and pulled back from Tom.

"*Now*, bro? Tom rolled his eyes.

"Yup."

Tom shook his head, smiling back at Savannah.

She gaped at both of them.

"You don't have to if − ?" Tom began.

"No... I mean, yes. I'd like to. But..." She frowned at him.

"Oh, I'm not going anywhere," he assured her, cottoning to her dilemma.

She became relieved and excited.

"You'd better lie down," Tom told Greg, who had continued to stroke Savannah with a feather-like touch.

As soon as Greg stood up straight, she realized how much agony he must be in, as his huge cock looked ready to burst. She scooted over while Tom stood up, and Greg lay down on his back, in the position she had previously been in, right in the center of the bed.

"Sit on top," Greg told her, holding out a hand to help her.

Savannah frowned. She'd never been allowed to try any positions other than missionary.

Tom smiled and helped her up. "Just straddle him," he explained, helping her lift one leg over Greg's thigh. He was a big guy, and she felt incredibly open as her legs stretched around his.

Greg's cock hovered around her pussy, tickling the inside of her thigh then touching her labia as she knelt over him.

Tom went to the drawer of one of the nightstands and took something from it, handing it to Greg before sitting on the bed beside him. He then wrapped his arms around Savannah's shoulders and crashed his lips against hers in an assuring but needy kiss.

She ran her hands through his hair as their kiss became more fervent, and she jumped when Greg caressed her wet pussy. Tom chuckled, knowing exactly what his friend was up to, and Savannah relaxed again as she enjoyed the ministrations of both her men.

Excitement rose within her as Tom's kiss became more demanding, and Greg's fingers slid in and out of her vagina. Her breath became ragged and her passion almost reached fever pitch as she snatched at Tom's hair, willing Greg to go further.

"Are you sure, sweetheart?" Greg tore a foil wrapper with his teeth, his fingers keeping up a steady rhythm inside her.

She nodded and made an affirmative noise in her throat, as her mouth was too full of Tom's tongue to speak.

Greg used his cock to brush over her clit, making her breath hitch before he placed it at her entrance.

"Your turn," Tom murmured, trailing kisses from her mouth to her ear.

She leaned forward while he steadied her.

"Whenever you're ready." Greg's voice was calm and controlled, which amazed her, seeing as he must have been desperate for his own release by now.

She enveloped the tip of his cock with her pussy and she sensed a slight pressure as she eased down on it. She'd had sex before, of course, but Daniel was way smaller than either of these guys. Tom wrapped his mouth around hers just as she bore down her weight, and she let out a guttural yelp as she welcomed Greg's cock into her. The pain was fleeting but the pleasure was exhilarating.

"You're in charge," Greg reminded her, lifting her thighs to help her ease upward.

Savannah had never been told that before, and she balked. Greg helped her lower her body back down, and she was surprised that there was absolutely no pain at all as she slid up and down his massive shaft. She had never experienced sensations like these before and gasped and moaned with delight. Tom continued to kiss her and nuzzle her neck and shoulders before licking his way down to her breast and taking a nipple into his mouth.

She had one arm around his shoulder, while she clung to Greg's bicep with her free hand. Everything felt different, new and delightful. The guys lavished her with care and adoration, whispering and murmuring compliments and words of encouragement.

"That's it, sweetheart. Ride me," Greg told her, his voice like gravel.

Tom sucked her nipple and her whole body tensed. Her folds seemed to suck Greg's cock farther into her as she became more and more aroused. Savannah lost control and grabbed at their flesh, screaming her release as she was overtaken with emotion and sensation, while Greg let out a roar as he exploded into the rubber sheath.

Biting down hard on Tom's shoulder, Savannah fought to silence herself. Her sudden fear of hurting him was allayed as soon as she heard his moan of pleasure.

"That's it! Harder!" he urged.

Savannah gasped in surprise. She frantically kissed the area she had just dug her teeth into, sure it must have throbbed like the devil. Confusion racked her as tears ran down her cheeks.

"It's all right. It's okay." Tom assured her, pulling her head up to face him.

He was blurry and it was dark, save for the TV flickering with color. The candles had burned down and the air was cooler. Tom put his hands either side of her face, forcing her to look at him.

She tried to calm herself as a myriad of emotions raced through her.

"It's all right," he told her again, his voice calm and kind.

With a sniff, she stared into his dark eyes. "But I—"

"You didn't hurt me."

"I…"

"It's all right."

"I love you, both of you." She looked from him to Greg, who was staring up at her.

"Oh, beautiful. We love you, too," Tom said, taking her in his arms once again. She buried her wet face in his shoulder.

"What he said," Greg piped up, making them both pull away and look back down at him.

Tom frowned. "I suppose you'd better move, bro."

Greg's cock was still inside her—and still quite big. "Well, I didn't want to spoil the moment," Greg replied with a smile.

"I'm so sorry," Savannah told him, moving off him.

"Don't be," Greg told her. "I'd stay there forever if I could."

"Yeah, I'd never get a look in if he had his way," Tom agreed, helping her off the bed and steadying her as her feet hit the floor.

She grabbed his arm as her knees almost buckled.

"Whoa!" Tom wrapped his other arm around her.

"I think it's my turn," Greg said, coming around the other side of the bed.

Tom relinquished his hold as Greg put both arms around her. "I love you," he whispered.

Savannah sank into his warmth as he kissed her gently, and Tom trailed his hand up her back.

"Let's try out the size of that new shower," Tom suggested as the credits ran up the TV screen.

Chapter Fifteen

Savannah was welcomed by the smell of fresh coffee the next morning, as Greg placed a cup on the nightstand.

"Morning, sleepyhead. Did you rest well?" His smile lit up her whole day.

"Yes, thank you." She beamed, sitting up in the empty bed. "You're up early."

"Some of us have work to do, including you," he told her with a wink. "Providing you're up to it, of course. How are you feeling?"

"A bit sore, but nothing I can't handle," she admitted.

He frowned. "Oh, no. We weren't too rough, were we?"

"No. It's just...been a while."

"Oh. Right."

"Morning, beautiful." Tom appeared in the doorway. "We'll have to go out for breakfast, I'm afraid — unless you want potato chips again?"

Savannah fidgeted then pulled out her hand. "No, thanks. I already have some." She grinned, holding them up to show him.

"Yeah, scratchy little fuckers, aren't they?" Greg grimaced.

"I did tell you not to spill them in the bed," Tom replied, rolling his eyes.

Savannah snickered. "What time do you have to be at the ranch?" She took a sip of coffee.

"In about an hour," Tom said.

"Which is about ten minutes after you need to be at work," Greg added.

"What?" She frowned, recalling that he'd mentioned something about that just now.

"Sandy rang. Apparently Mrs. Taylor's leg's hurting her, so she's cancelled her hair appointment this morning," Greg said, while Tom rifled through one of the bags he'd brought over yesterday.

"And that means…?"

"Two things," he told her. "Firstly, she's got time to speak to you about that job she promised you."

She raised her eyebrows. "And…?"

"Secondly, she needs you to go over to Mrs. Taylor's house later and fix her hair for her, part of that mobile business we were talking about." Greg looked like the cat that had eaten the canary.

Savannah smiled. Things couldn't be going any better for her. "I'd better get up, then," she said.

"Here. These shouldn't be too bad," Tom said, throwing a pile of clothes onto the end of the bed. "We'll need to see about getting you some new clothes later."

Savannah's heart sank. "I should've gotten them last night while I had the chance," she said.

"No, you shouldn't have," he told her. "You didn't want anything from that house and we totally agree with you. Leave everything behind, memories and all. We'll get you some lovely new clothes from a place in town where Isla Gillingham shops."

"The model?" She gaped.

"Yup. She lives not far from here," Greg piped up. "Carla told us about her. She's been in the shop a few times—a real nice lady, apparently."

"Oh my God! She's gorgeous," Savannah gushed. "I heard about her on the radio, and I saw her pictures in a magazine when I was in the doctor's waiting room once. Have you met her?"

"Not yet," Greg replied, "but, to be fair, we don't get out much."

"So far we haven't, though I've a feeling that's about to change," Tom added. "And talking of changing, we'd best let you get into those clothes if we're gonna get a chance of some breakfast before that interview." He raised his eyes at Savannah, who beamed.

"There's a spare toothbrush in the bathroom cabinet, and use whatever you need," Greg told her as the guys headed toward the door.

* * * *

It wasn't long before Savannah was ready and they all piled into a booth at the nearby café. The guys hadn't exaggerated about the grumpiness of the owner, and Savannah marveled at how he'd managed to stay open at all while being so unfriendly.

He was probably in his late fifties, with gray hair and a scowl that could turn milk sour. His arm was in a sling and he used his one free hand to flick through the morning paper that had been spread across the counter when they'd arrived. He'd huffed when he saw them, which wasn't hard, as they were his only customers. With all the effort of a hippo trying to run from a standing start, he lumbered around the side of the counter to approach them.

"I can't cook," he snapped, pointing to the sling.

"We know. We've eaten here before," Greg mumbled.

Savannah put a hand in front of her face to hide a snigger.

"And I can't hear. You'll have to speak up."

She sagged with relief.

"Can you do toast and coffee?" Greg said, annunciating the words clearly.

The man narrowed his eyes, unsure whether Greg was making fun of him or not. He grunted and sauntered back to the counter.

"Maybe we can eat at the diner in town," Tom suggested.

"And spoil all the fun? Where's your sense of adventure, bud?" Greg smirked.

Savannah couldn't help giggling.

Tom rolled his eyes. "Well, he'd better not take all day over it, or we'll all be late for work."

It didn't take long for him to cook the toast and pour three cups of coffee.

"I'll come over," Tom offered and placed it all on a tray to carry across. "Thank you," he said, offering him the cash.

The old guy grunted again and Tom returned to the booth.

"This is nice," Savannah chirped, spreading jam on her toast.

"Really?" Tom looked aghast.

"Having breakfast with you guys. And...you know" — she lowered her voice — "last night."

Greg hooted, and Tom grinned.

"How are you feeling?" Tom asked.

"Fine, thank you."

"Good." He winked at her and she blushed. "How about moving in with us permanently — unless it's a bit too soon?"

She gaped at him. "Seriously?"

Tom sniggered. "Yup."

"Oh, unless his snoring's put you off," Greg piped up. "I did warn you about that. It can break the sound barrier on a really bad night."

"Ha-ha, very funny," Tom said.

Just then, his phone rang and he pulled it from his pocket. "It's the boss," he said with a grimace.

"We're not late," Greg said, checking his watch.

"Morning, Matt. Is everything okay?" Tom frowned, answering the call. "No, we're at the café near our place at Bracken Ridge." He looked over at Savannah then indicated that he'd take the call outside.

"So, what do you think?" Greg asked.

Savannah watched Tom leave. "What?"

"About moving in. I was just kidding about Tom's snoring, by the way. Though we can always get earplugs, just in case. Don't tell him I said that, though."

She stared up at him for a second, computing what he was talking about. "Oh, yeah. I mean...yeah, I'd love to move in with you, if you're sure?"

"Of course." He smiled, taking her hands across the table. "Sweetheart, we meant what we said last night. We love you. We want to be with you. And I know Mrs. H is a lovely lady, but we really can't — "

"I get it." She laughed. Then she put her hand to her mouth in horror. "Oh, no, I should have called her last night when I didn't go back there. She might've worried."

"Of course, she'd have worried," Greg said. "That's why I rang her while you were in the shower. The *first* shower. I told her we were heading over to Upton Crossing so we weren't sure how late we'd be. We thought it best to stay over at our house to save disturbing her when we got back. She was cool." He smiled.

"Thank you. I should've thought…"

"You had enough to think about, as I recall," he told her, "so don't look so concerned."

She smiled, relief sweeping over her.

The door banged and Tom returned, his eyes wide. "Well, that was interesting."

"I'll bet it was." Greg nodded. "So are you gonna tell us or are we playing twenty questions here?"

Tom shook his head wearily as he sat next to Savannah. "Matt was checking that we weren't eating in the diner this morning. Dyson had to let Bramhall and Edgerton go, pending court proceedings. He's got a load of intel on that firm they're working for and guess who owns it? They do."

Savannah gasped. "What?"

"You might not wanna hear this, beautiful," Tom said, placing a hand on her shoulder.

"You may as well hit me with it," she said, figuring it couldn't be that bad.

"He's mortgaged your house to the hilt to pay for his share of the business," Tom said, "although Pete Bramhall has the larger share."

Savannah shook her head. "It's okay. I said goodbye to my inheritance a long time ago when he first used it as the deposit," she said. "I knew that whatever happened, I'd never see that money again."

"Doesn't make it right, though," Greg said through gritted teeth.

"There's something else, too," Tom said.

"I thought there might be," Greg replied.

"Remember when we had that meeting and we insisted on some kind of testimonials about the supplements?"

"Yeah."

"They finally gave in and gave us the name and number of a guy to contact?"

"The one that went straight to voicemail." Greg rolled his eyes, taking the last sip of his coffee.

"Remember the name?" Tom's eyes shone.

Greg looked blank.

"Ben Hathaway."

The penny dropped, as did Greg's jaw.

Savannah frowned. *Why does that name ring a bell?*

"As in Belinda Hathaway? That woman we left digging up flowers from the front garden last night?" Greg gaped.

"The very same. She'd left Ben a couple of weeks ago to live with her mother—or so he thought." Tom shook his head, incredulous.

"So, she was cheating, too?" Savannah suddenly perceived the woman she'd felt sorry for the previous night in a much different way.

"Ben worked for Stone Supplements, but in a clerical capacity. They own a small holding over at Jacobstown, apparently," Tom went on.

"So, they'd send us over there if they had to, to see the results of these 'miracle supplements', I suppose." Greg used his fingers as quotation marks.

"Yeah, even though he probably doesn't use them," Tom said with a snigger.

"Not if he's got any sense." Greg added.

"If he had any sense, he wouldn't be working for them in the first place," Savannah piped up.

"She's got a good point, there, bro," Tom said.

"Yup. Well, we'd better head on over there. Matt wasn't checking up on us, was he? Thinking we'd be late or something?" Greg stood up.

"No, nothing like that." Tom shook his head, standing slowly. "In fact, he said we can take our time. He's not at the ranch right now. He'll be there later. He just wanted to let us know what was happening and also to warn us."

Greg frowned. "About what?"

Savannah went hot with worry.

"Well, you know I said Dyson had to let those fuckwads go while he gathered more evidence for court? They were last seen in the diner at Pelican's Heath." Tom slung an arm around Savannah and they left the café.

"What the hell are they doing, hanging around? They've got no business here." Greg seethed as he followed Savannah into the truck.

"Beats me." Tom started the engine. "But we don't want any trouble. Remember?"

"I hear ya." Greg didn't sound too convincing.

Savannah snuggled up to him. "They're not worth it," she said.

"That's right, beautiful," Tom agreed, taking a hand off the steering wheel to stroke her cheek.

"I know," Greg said, pursing his lips. "It just makes me so mad."

"Will I see you later? After work, I mean?" Savannah asked.

"Of course." Tom frowned. "You do want to move in, don't you?"

"Oh, yes. I just didn't know when you'd —"

"The sooner the better, I reckon," Greg interjected, perking up all of a sudden.

"We'll drop in to pick up the rest of our stuff from Mrs. H's later and settle the bill 'til the end of the week. Then we can all go back to Bracken Ridge." Tom sounded more cheerful, too.

"She'll be glad. She needs the rooms for her guests next week," Savannah said with a smile.

"We might need to fetch a few supplies on the way home, too, come to think of it," Greg added.

"Yeah, and you can change the bedding tonight, don't forget," Tom said, shaking his head. "We don't all want to be scratched by those dang potato chips again."

Greg sniggered. "You've got a point, there, buddy."

They pulled up in the main street of Pelican's Heath, just outside the hair salon. Savannah suddenly had butterflies in her stomach.

"Do I look okay?" she asked Greg as he helped her out of the truck.

"You look gorgeous," he assured her. "Though we might have to think about finding that fancy boutique as soon as we can or Tom'll run out of clothes to wear."

"*I'm* not wearing clothes from some fancy boutique," Tom said with a jovial frown as he came around the side of the truck.

"For *me*, silly." Savannah giggled, feeling much more relaxed.

"Oh, right. Come on. Let's get this interview over with, then." Tom went ahead and opened the door of the hairdresser's.

"Are you coming with me?" Savannah frowned.

"Of course. We wanna make sure you're not taken advantage of," Greg told her. "Well, not by the customers, anyway," he added with a wink.

"We want to see if you'll need transporting anywhere," Tom clarified, shaking his head at his buddy as they walked in. "We can arrange your mobile jobs around our work if we need to."

"There's no need for that," Sandy called to them from the back wash. "Most of the ladies are in town, anyway. Though there might be some evening work involved, if that's all right? We can figure it out as we go, though." She beamed at them, waving a flippant hand.

"Great." Savannah smiled back at her. "I'm not late, am I?" She was concerned that Sandy had been washing someone's hair after saying she'd be free this morning because of Mrs. Taylor's cancellation.

"Oh no, dear. I'm not a proper customer," the older lady said from the chair where Sandy had just finished washing her hair.

"This is Delores. She and Frank run the general store," Sandy explained.

"Where Carla works," Tom clarified.

"Oh, yes. I've been in there. It's very nice," Savannah told her.

"Thank you, dear." Delores smiled. "You must be Savannah."

"Yes."

"My new member of the staff," Sandy added, wrapping a towel around Delores' hair.

"Oh, good. That'll certainly take some of the pressure off you," Delores told Sandy.

"Pressure? The day I start feeling pressured is the day I hang up my scissors for good, lady," Sandy said with a laugh.

"And so you should," Delores agreed with a smile.

"Well, if we're not needed, I guess we'll head on over to the ranch," Greg said before taking Savannah in his arms for a kiss.

Tom followed suit, leaving Savannah breathless as they headed for the door.

"We'll try to drop in later," Greg called from the doorway. "Maybe take you for lunch?"

"That would be lovely." Savannah beamed as they left.

"Well now, I'll have what she just had, please," Delores said to Sandy before they all laughed.

The phone rang and Sandy went to answer it, offering Delores a comb.

"I just popped in to get my hair washed," Delores explained to Savannah. "I'm getting a little old to do it myself and my hands don't move as much as they used to. It's so much easier to just sit back and let someone else do it for me." She gave a self-deprecating laugh.

"Here, let me comb it for you," Savannah offered.

Delores looked surprised. "Well, that's very kind, but I'm not exactly what you'd call a paying customer, hon. I just popped in while it was quiet, you know."

"Then let me do it for you as a friend," Savannah said warmly, taking the comb from her. "Why don't you sit over there where it's a little warmer? "She indicated a chair that sat opposite a large mirror. A radiator ran along the wall beside it.

"I think you're gonna fit in just fine around here," Delores declared, settling into the soft chair.

Savannah took a thick towel from a nearby shelf and wrapped it around Delores' shoulders before gently combing through her wet hair. Then she picked up a hairdryer.

"Oh, I'm not having the full works, hon. I just came for a quick wash," Delores insisted.

"It's far too cold to go out there with wet hair," Savannah said. "You'll catch your death."

"Well, if you're sure?"

"Of course."

Savannah took a round brush and styled Delores's hair in no time.

"Well, don't you look great?" Sandy returned, smiling.

Delores beamed in the mirror. "Frank won't recognize me when I get back," she laughed. "I love it." She swished her head from side to side, admiring her look.

"I'm glad you like it." Savannah had a warm feeling in her stomach and a broad smile on her face.

"Well, you've definitely got a job here for as long as you want it," Sandy told her. "Now, how about I show you where we make the coffee around here and we can talk through the particulars? I just spoke to Josie over at the Fielding Ranch and she's got quite a few ladies needing their hair styled before her party next week. I don't know where we'll put 'em all, but I'm sure we'll manage." She looked around the tiny salon with a sigh.

"Maybe we could go to them?" Savannah suggested. "If they don't need anything too specialized, I'm sure we could take some equipment over."

"She's got a good idea there," Delores said, raising her eyebrows.

Sandy beamed. "That's exactly why I hired her."

Chapter Sixteen

"They're looking a lot better, ain't they?" Greg's breath could be seen in the cold air as he gestured toward the cattle in the field. "Despite not having any of those supplements." He snickered.

"*Because* they didn't have any, you mean?" Tom said. "There's no telling what's in those things." The thought made him sick.

"Dyson'll find out," Greg told him, "and if it's anything untoward, they'll be up on even bigger charges."

"You think they'll both get slung in jail over a few dud cow pills?" Tom shook his head.

"They'll have to do *some* time for fraud and deception, I reckon. There'll be tax evasion and all sorts of stuff mixed up with that, for sure."

Tom bit his lip, hammering the last stake in a little harder than was necessary.

Greg was kneeling down, collecting the tools and putting them in a leather bag. He frowned. "That's not all that's bothering you, is it, buddy?"

"I wanna see them do time for what they've done, especially that fuckwad Edgerton."

"You mean for fraud or for what he's done to Savannah?"

Tom stared at the ground. "Both."

"We've got no proof he did anything," Greg said with a sigh. "I mean, we know he beat her, but that won't stand up in court. She never reported it."

"You saw that scar." Tom clenched the hammer. "It was a weird shape, too, not just like a regular cut that could've been an accident. It had a curve to it, as well. That's got to be deliberate."

Greg stood, nodding. "I saw it. We can't just come out and ask her about it, though. You know how she is. She'll clam up on us."

"Yeah, well, maybe we should all start opening up a little. Get everything out in the open." Tom threw the hammer into the tool bag.

"You wanna tell her about Beth?"

Tom pursed his lips. "She needs to know. About me, I mean. What I did."

"I miss Beth too, buddy," Greg said. "But you don't need to beat yourself up over it. What happened to her was tragic, but we can't change that."

"No, but I shouldn't have —"

"Forget it. You can't alter the past."

Tom huffed.

"Looks like Matt's back," Greg said, looking toward the house where a truck had just pulled up. "Let's hope he's got some news."

"Don't hold your breath on that score," Tom mumbled, picking up a coil of rope and following his friend.

"Hey, guys." Matt smiled as they walked over to him. "Are they all safe and sound now?"

"It'll take more than a hurricane to knock that fence down," Greg said with a grin. "Tom's made extra sure of that."

Tom snorted. Taking out his aggression on the fence posts was the best way to do it, in his book. Pity, though. He'd been in a good mood this morning when he'd arrived at the ranch. But seeing those cattle and how badly they'd been treated had taken his mind right back to Savannah and that bastard husband of hers. Knowing that he was free and roaming around the town was just too much.

"Has the sheriff locked those fuckers up again yet?" Tom asked.

Matt grimaced. "No, but he's working on it. In fact, he said he might need statements from you guys later, just to confirm what happened at that meeting over at Upton."

"With pleasure," Tom assured him.

Matt nodded. "Great." He checked his watch. "Either of you got time to bank some cash for me before you head off for lunch? I'd appreciate the favor. Aiden Fielding's asked me to go see about Josie's party and I won't make it to Almondine in time."

"I'll go," Tom offered, figuring he could do with some time on his own to let off some steam.

"Thanks. There's not much, but time's just slipping away from me today." Matt reached into his truck and pulled out a large envelope. "It's all in there."

"No worries." Tom took the package and turned back to Greg. "I'll meet you over at the diner as soon as I get back."

Greg nodded, and Tom headed for their truck.

* * * *

Savannah was having a lovely morning at the salon, and her new boss seemed impressed with her work.

"It's a good thing you were here today," Sandy said when they stopped for a break. "Mrs. Taylor was really pleased with your visit and you've been a massive help here. Business is really picking up. How about doing some nails this afternoon?"

"I'd love to. It's been a while since I did many, though, so I might be a bit rusty." She grimaced. "I don't even paint my own anymore."

Sandy laughed. "Nothing worse than rusty nails, eh?" She looked over at Savannah's hands and smiled. "You keep yours well-manicured, though. You could paint them if you wanted to, surely?"

Savannah didn't want to admit that her husband had forbidden her from painting her nails as he said they looked tarty and cheap. Besides, spending all her time doing housework instead of working or socializing meant it was more practical to keep them short and plain. She'd enjoyed learning all about nail care and painting, as well as what she regarded as 'the fun stuff' — how to set gems, color blocking, along with intricate nail art — so it would be good to put it all into practice again.

"I will, now that I'm working here," she replied with a smile. "And I'm going to get some new clothes soon. My own got ruined." She looked down at the large sweater and jeans that she had borrowed from Tom. He'd made an extra hole in one of his belts so she could hoist the Levi's around her waist, and she'd rolled up the hems. She wore a large T-shirt underneath the sweater and a couple of extra pairs of socks to make his boots stay on her feet. She was beginning to regret leaving her clothes at Upton Crossing.

Her long red hair was tied in a ponytail and she mused about the different styles she could try for work. It was exciting to have a reason to smarten herself up again.

"How about some lunch while it's quiet?" Sandy suggested. "Didn't those guys of yours mention something about the diner?"

Savannah hadn't forgotten. She was looking forward to it. Greg had rung earlier to say that they'd try to make it for about half past one, and it was twenty past already. "I'd better get over there," she said, smoothing a few stray hairs from her face.

"Take as long as you like." Sandy smiled.

"Thanks. I shouldn't be too long."

Savannah pulled on Tom's old Carhartt and headed outside. The diner was only across the road, so she didn't have to brave the cold for too long. Winter sure had arrived.

The diner was quite busy, and she was disappointed the guys weren't already there, though she was early. She found a spare table near the window and sat down, embarrassed that she couldn't even afford a coffee while she waited. Everyone seemed very friendly, though, and several smiled over at her.

A young girl with long blonde hair and big blue eyes approached her. Savannah noticed how beautiful she looked, with perfect make-up and what appeared to be a designer dress and jacket, with a large handbag.

"Hi. You're not Savannah Edgerton, are you?"

Savannah raised her eyebrows in surprise. "Yes."

The girl smiled, taking the seat opposite her. "I thought so."

"And you are...?" Savannah frowned.

"I'm Frankie." She beamed.

Savannah's stomach thudded. This was the girl who had cheated on her guys and she was gorgeous. She narrowed her eyes. "How do you know me?"

Frankie shrugged. "Just a guess. I haven't seen you before, so I knew you must be new in town. I know everyone. You've been seeing Greg Jackson and Tom Rankin, haven't you?"

Savannah scanned the room, willing the guys to arrive. There was no sign of them. "How do you know that?" *Have they been talking about me? To her, of all people?*

She snorted. "Everyone knows everything in a town like this. It's okay. I'm not going to take them back or anything." Frankie's pious attitude grated like fingernails down a blackboard.

"I know." Savannah longed to tell her that she was well aware the guys had turned her down, but she bit her lip...for now.

Frankie's jaw tightened and she looked at Savannah's attire disparagingly. Savannah shuddered.

"They're just a couple of desperate cowboys," Frankie said on a sigh. "I'm glad I saw their true colors when I did."

Savannah's blood boiled and she chewed her lip. "What's that supposed to mean?" She wasn't sure she wanted to hear what the bitch had to say, but she had to admit to being intrigued.

Frankie sat back, putting her hand to her mouth as though astonished. "Oh, no. You don't know about them, do you?"

"Know what?" Her teeth were clenched.

"About their violence, the criminal record, the grievous bodily harm charge, the jail sentence. Oh, no, you really are naïve, aren't you?" Frankie was clearly enjoying herself, but Savannah was furious.

"That's not true!"

Frankie gave her a mock-sympathetic smile. "Sorry, doll. It's all in here." She pulled a newspaper out of her bag. "I fetched this to show a couple of guys who were asking about them earlier. Looks like they already left, though. They said they had to get over to Almondine on some business." She shrugged, then held it up.

Thug Jailed for Serious Assault. The headline spoke for itself.

"I was going out with them, so my daddy ran a check at the newspaper office. He's in charge over there. This article was in a paper from over at Pinebridge County, where the incident happened. Right outside the court house, it was, in full view of everyone. There's pictures and everything." She offered the paper to Savannah.

She didn't need to see it. Somehow she knew this self-righteous, smarmy bitch was telling the truth. Jumping to her feet, she stormed out of the diner as hot, heavy tears started to stream down her face. As she blindly ran down the street, she almost ran into a familiar cowboy.

"Hey, there you are. Sorry, I'm a bit late, but— Savannah? What's happened?" Greg had his arms around her in a flash, but she pushed against his muscular frame.

"Don't you dare touch me! Just leave me alone!"

"What? Why?" He let go, holding his hands up to pacify her. "Savannah, what's all this about?"

"I *know*," she screeched at him, digging her finger into his chest. "I thought you were kind and loving, but you were just using me. You're nothing but a violent bastard, just like Daniel. You're all the fucking same!"

"You're wrong." He grabbed her arms. "Savannah, I don't know what you've heard, but you need to listen to me." His voice was firm, though he didn't shout.

"I haven't just heard. I've *seen*!" she hollered between sobs. "It's there in black and white. You're a fucking jailbird, nothing but a common criminal. A thug!"

He was holding her tightly now, and she knew he was willing her to stop yelling, but she couldn't. It needed to be said.

"I believed you, every word you said. I thought you were both honest and kind and all the time you were leading me on. You're as bad as Daniel, lying and cheating and—"

"That's enough." His sudden outburst shocked her into silence as he clenched her arms even tighter. "Now, I don't know who told you all this stuff, but you've got it totally wrong. We've never lied to you, I promise."

"Jailbird!" She bit the word from her mouth.

"For your information, it wasn't *me* who went to jail," he told her abruptly.

She stared at him, blinking away the tears.

He huffed, looking around at the people who had stopped to watch them. Savannah noticed their audience for the first time. She had never made a scene before. Yelling in the street was unheard of.

"Let's go and talk somewhere quiet," he said. "The diner's just down here. We can—"

She turned to see what had stopped him talking. Frankie was just coming out of the diner. She gave them a smarmy smile when she saw them and tapped her bag.

"I might have guessed." Greg seethed. He turned back to Savannah. "You've been talking to Frankie, haven't you?"

She nodded. He was furious but curbed his emotions well.

Frankie walked off in the opposite direction.

"I'm guessing she told you about the scene outside the courthouse, huh? Showed you that damn newspaper?"

"Yeah." Seeing him so angry somehow calmed her down. "Are you going to deny it?" Her voice was quieter now.

"Nope. It happened all right. Tom hit that guy. Unfortunately, he did it at the wrong time and place and got jailed for it, but he was only doing what any decent person would have done, what I'd have done myself if he hadn't gotten there first." Greg's lips were tight.

Savannah's heart pumped against her ribs. She'd wanted him to deny it, to tell her it was all a mistake and the papers had gotten it wrong. *She'd* gotten it wrong. But she hadn't. For once, she was right on the money...unfortunately.

"Why don't we get that coffee?" she suggested.

He nodded and put an arm around her as they went to the diner.

"You want some lunch?" he asked her when they reached the counter.

"No, I'm not hungry."

They took their drinks and sat at a quiet table in the corner.

"Tom wanted to tell you himself," Greg said. "He's ashamed that he was so stupid and ended up in jail for it. That jailbird tag's gonna follow him for the rest of his life like a millstone around his neck. But I still think he was right to do it."

"Violence is never acceptable." She took a sip of her drink, her stomach churning. She didn't want to believe that either of her guys could be capable of something like that, never mind condone it.

"Maybe not. But in some circumstances, it's all you've got." He toyed with a teaspoon as she stared at him. She'd never thought he'd say anything like that.

"I don't know you," she murmured. "Either of you."

He grabbed her hand just as she was about to stand up and leave.

"Listen to me."

She gaped.

"We had a lovely girl, Beth Coulter. She was a beautiful, young, happy woman with a brilliant future ahead of her. A future with us, we'd hoped. We'd been seeing her for a few months. We fell in love. Each of us had a good job, prospects, everything to live for. Then, one dark, rainy night, Beth left her job at the hospital to come home to us." He paused, taking a long sip of his drink.

Savannah dreaded what was to come next.

"She was just crossing the road when a car skidded around the corner and ran right into her. Killed her outright. The driver was drunk. He didn't even know what he'd done until the next day and he didn't care." Greg spat out the last sentence.

"Oh my God. I'm so sorry."

Tears were in his eyes when he looked at her, and she squeezed his hand. "We loved her." He sniffed. "It was the first time we'd loved anyone like that."

"It must have been awful." She didn't know what to say. Greg looked so sad that she just wanted to hold him, but she got the impression there was more to his story. And if he didn't tell it now, he never would.

"Part of us died with her that night. We just couldn't get our heads right. It didn't feel true." Greg wiped his eye.

"But they got him? The man who killed her?"

He nodded. "Oh yeah, they got him all right. Chuck Turner, fucking shitbag. He showed no remorse. The only thing he was sorry about was getting caught." He sniffed again. "He tried to make out that she just stepped out in front of him. He said she was following some stray dog that had run into the road and she ran after it, not looking for traffic. She left him no choice. He couldn't stop."

"Oh, no!"

"She was a nurse, for fuck's sake. She knew how to cross a damn road."

"But he was drunk."

"That's the only thing they actually got him on — driving while over the limit. His fancy lawyers got him off on a charge of drunk driving and manslaughter, not murder. They found some stray dog walking the area, so they concocted the story that it was the one she was trying to save. She was a hero and should have been commended for her kindness, was what they said. The fact she was a nurse was the icing on the cake. It just went to prove what a magnanimous person she was. It backed up his story perfectly. He even claimed that he managed to maneuver his car to avoid running over the dog but didn't see her until it was too late. That was supposed to prove that although he'd had too much to drink, he still had all his faculties. Yeah, right. Convenient that there were no witnesses to any of it." He pressed his lips together, frustrated as well as angry.

"But that's so unfair." Savannah had tears streaming down her cheeks again.

"Tell me about it." He took another sip of his drink.

"So, that's why Tom hit him?"

Greg snorted. "Tom hit the bastard because after he'd gotten off on a lighter sentence — thanks to his expensive legal team — he had the nerve to shout '*she should have been more careful*' just as they were taking him down. He was looking right at us with this smug leer."

"Oh, no."

Greg gave a self-deprecating smile. "It was madness. We didn't think. We hightailed it after him. One of the guards held me back, but Tom managed to squeeze through his entourage and thump him right in the face. Broke his nose. Of course, Tom was immediately arrested."

"But he was provoked. You both were." Savannah was horrified.

"And that fucker was rich. He managed to get Tom charged with assault. At first, it looked like he was going to jail — hence the paper's take on it — but he just spent a night in the cell before the judge acknowledged it was a provoked attack and he got off with a hefty fine and community service. Spent a whole summer working in the laundry of the local hospital. Hot and heavy work, but he learned how to fold sheets properly."

Savannah wiped her face with a snigger. "That explains his concerns about potato chips in the bed, then."

Greg smiled.

"Where is he, by the way? I thought he'd be with you?" Savannah felt a little better as she looked around the half-empty diner. The lunch rush was over and there were just a few customers sitting around drinking coffee.

"He had to go to the bank for Matt. He shouldn't be long. It's only in Almondine." Greg finished his drink.

Savannah immediately heated. "He— He's gone to Almondine?"

"Yup."

"I think that's where Daniel is."

Greg shot to his feet, kicking his chair backward. "We'll have to borrow Carla's truck. I got a ride here with Dyson."

They ran out of the diner and up the street to the little general store. Delores was standing behind the counter, while Carla was neatly stacking tins of tuna.

"Carla, have you got your pickup?"

She raised her eyebrows, standing up. "Yeah. You need it?" She pulled the keys from her jeans pocket, offering them to him.

"Thanks." He nodded, and they whizzed back out of the door to where a blue truck stood at the side of the building.

"D'you think Tom'll say anything?" Savannah's heart pounded as she climbed in and shut the door.

"There's only one way to find out." Greg put his foot to the floor and they sped out of town.

Chapter Seventeen

Tom felt much better by the time he reached the bank. He'd driven with the window open, despite the cold, and some cheery Alan Jackson hits blaring from the speakers.

Almondine was busy, as usual, and he had to drive around a while to find somewhere to park the truck. He didn't like this town much. It wasn't just bigger and busier than Pelican's Heath. The people here didn't seem half as friendly. Everyone was always rushing with their business, never stopping for a chat or even a hello.

One reason he'd loved living in Pinebridge was that the folks had been so friendly and laid back out there. That was, until that bastard Chuck Turner had arrived and ruined everything.

He shook his head, trying to clear the unpleasant thoughts from his mind. He'd always miss Beth, but it was time to put it all behind him. They were in Cavern

County now and had lots of friends in Pelican's Heath already.

It had been too much to expect their past not to follow them, and, of course, it had to be Frankie — or at least her dad — who'd dug the dirt. The locals didn't seem to mind so much, though, the few who knew about it anyhow. Matt Shearer had been happy to offer them work, even with his tarnished legal record, and the guys both loved their jobs. And now they had Savannah to love, too. He smiled at the thought as he made his way to the large bank.

The line was nearly to the door when he walked into the building and people were already grumbling and checking their watches while they waited. He wasn't in that much of a hurry, though he was looking forward to meeting up with Savannah at the diner a little later. He hoped she was having a good time with Sandy and the ladies who frequented that hair salon. There was always plenty of gossip there, and Savannah would soon get to know everyone.

He peered at the plain walls of the old building. It was the only bank for miles, so it was always crowded. Matt had mentioned something about them building one at Pelican's Heath, as the town was growing much bigger now, apparently. He hoped that was right. It sure would save a lot of time traveling and waiting around.

Eventually, he made it to the front of the line and handed over the money and deposit chit. The teller didn't even crack a smile as she processed it and handed him the receipt without a word.

"Thanks very much. You have a great day, won't you?" He smiled at her and she looked stunned. With a snigger, he left the bank and sighed with relief as the cold air hit him again. He was about to head for the truck when he heard something that made his blood boil.

"Hey, jailbird. You been robbin' the bank now?"

He spun on his heel and seethed as Daniel Edgerton came sauntering toward him, a sneer on his ugly face.

Tom tucked the receipt in his pocket, leaving his hands free, and cracked his knuckles as the fuckwad got closer.

"Are you talking to me, Edgerton?" His words were clipped.

Daniel opened his eyes wide. Then he looked up and down the street before facing Tom again. "Well, I don't see no other jailbirds around here, do you?"

"Well now, didn't you just spend the night in a police cell yourself?" Tom straightened his back, towering over his nemesis.

Daniel's lips tightened to a thin line. "Are you denying being arrested for showing what a thug you really are?" His smarmy tone was already getting on Tom's last nerve.

Tom clenched his fists but kept them firmly by his sides. He had to think of the consequences this time. It wasn't worth getting into more shit over a fuckwad like Edgerton, not after what had happened before. He didn't mind the hard graft — he was well used to that — but the stigma attached to having a criminal record rankled, and he knew it hadn't done Greg's reputation any good, either. He was shocked his friend had still wanted to associate with him after that, but Greg was loyal and Tom appreciated that more than anything.

"You're a fine one to talk on that subject. Now, get out of my sight and stay out." He turned his back on the troublemaker and took two steps down the street before the guy started hollering at him.

"You can't take the truth, can you, jailbird? You got busted for being the violent bastard that you are and you don't like it. Well, what do all these nice new neighbors of yours think about having a criminal in their midst?"

After taking a deep breath, Tom slowly turned around. Several passers-by had stopped to listen and were now murmuring and whispering among themselves. *Fuck!*

"All right. I hit a guy who provoked me. He was a good-for-nothing shithead who killed an innocent girl. Sound familiar?" His voice was deep and his words deliberate. Not shouting. Not losing control.

Daniel's face clouded over and his chest heaved with fury. "What the hell is that supposed to mean?"

The crowd was growing and the murmurs grew louder.

Tom enjoyed a fleeting air of self-satisfaction. Edgerton was riled. He'd hit a nerve.

"What do you think it means, fuckwad?" Tom put his hands on his hips, standing proud.

The tic in Daniel's neck jumped wildly and his face was bright red. "I've never killed anyone!" His voice was higher than usual, more like a squeak.

"Not yet."

"*Now* who's being provocative?" he sneered.

"If you can't take it, then don't dish it out, shithead."

"What do you mean by that?"

"What do you think I mean?"

Daniel curled his lip. "Are you implying that I'm some kind of wife beater?"

"Are you denying it? You practically admitted it in front of the sheriff. We all heard you."

There were audible gasps from the assembled crowd.

"She is a liar!"

"I don't think so." Tom became even calmer as Daniel got more agitated.

"And you should know, I suppose? You *are* the one sleeping with my wife, I take it?" Daniel looked even more pious as the crowd became more vocal.

Tom shook his head. "I haven't had intercourse with your wife. But I hear you've been sleeping around with the wife of one of your work colleagues. Said she was planning to marry you, even have kids with you. I don't suppose either of you had considered getting a divorce beforehand, had you?"

There were titters from some of the ladies standing nearby and Daniel narrowed his eyes at them. Then he stared back at Tom. "Is that what you want? Me to divorce the bitch? So *you* can have her?" His lips curved into a sneer. "Well, you can forget it. She's mine, d'you hear? *Mine.* Even if she's not with me, I *own* her."

The crowd fell silent.

"She's not a possession." Tom's blood boiled again and he fought to keep his cool as a heinous thought crossed his mind. "She's not something you stamp your name on and stake your claim to." He watched for his opponent's reaction. He wasn't disappointed.

Daniel's eyes flashed with triumph. "And what's wrong with marking my possessions? That's how everyone knows what belongs to me. My personalized registration plate, the key to my house..." He pulled out his initialed key fob to prove his point. "So, why not my wife?"

Tom's eyebrows knitted together as he stared with horror and incredulity. "The scar."

Daniel wore the same smug look that Chad Turner had worn after his session in court.

"You recognized it, then? Stupid bitch moved before I'd got it finished, but I'll have her branded, you mark my words."

Tom took a step toward the fuckwad, who slowly took a few steps back. "You tried to *carve* your initial into your wife's *flesh*?" He spat the words out as bile rose in his throat.

There were gasps and shrieks from the people around them.

Daniel's reply was a supercilious sneer.

Tom's fists clenched even harder as his heart hammered. He had to fight his every instinct not to kill the fucker on the spot.

"You bastard!" Someone ran through the crowd and grabbed Daniel by the throat. Greg. The throng around them started yelling, almost crushing each other to get closer to the action.

"Leave him!" Tom tried to haul his friend away, well aware of how his buddy felt.

"All right, Greg." Dyson suddenly appeared behind them with another officer. "You know it won't do any good."

"It might do *me* some fucking good!" Greg spat in Daniel's face. "You're a sick fucking monster, you know that?" he yelled.

"And what about Savannah? What good would it do *her*?" Tom asked, prying Greg's fingers from the bastard's neck.

Greg's muscular frame went lax as he relinquished his grip, and the sheriff started reading Edgerton his rights while the fuckwad gasped for breath.

Tom placed a comforting arm around Greg's shoulder, turning around to hear the mob cheering and whooping at them. Dyson and his colleague hauled their prisoner through the crowd to the sheriff's car, leaving the two guys staring in astonishment and relief.

"Hang the fucking bastard!" someone yelled as the squad car drove away. The remark was followed by lots of similar sentiments as others joined in.

"Where is she?" Tom looked around, feeling panicked.

Greg was still panting. "She was with me." He started searching, too.

People were hemming them in, patting them on the back and congratulating them on a job well done.

"You should've killed the bastard," a man told Greg.

"Fucking good thing I wasn't any closer," another one chimed in. "Well done, boys. Great job."

But the guys didn't feel triumphant, just sick.

"I told her about Beth," Greg mumbled.

"And me?"

"Yup."

"And?"

"Then we came here."

Tom shook his head. "What? She didn't say anything?"

"There wasn't time. She asked after you. I told her you were over here. Then she said that Edgerton had headed this way, too, so we got our asses straight here." Greg frowned. "I guess Carla must've alerted Dyson something was wrong. We borrowed her truck."

"Good thing he got here when he did. We almost both ended up with a criminal record." Tom rolled his eyes as they wandered through the last of the dispersing crowd, still receiving pats on the back.

"Hmm, I reckon one laundry maid in the family's enough." Greg snickered.

"Aren't you funny." Tom looked up the street and spotted Savannah waiting by the truck that looked like it had been abandoned in the middle of the road. Greg obviously hadn't been able to find a parking space, either. "There she is. D'you think she still wants us?"

The guys stood still to assess the situation. Her face was tearstained, and she was staring over at them. She was beautiful. They couldn't take their eyes off her but dared not take a step closer, not yet.

"I'd just convinced her you weren't a thug then showed her that *I* was one," Greg mumbled.

"You didn't hit him."

"And I told her that we loved Beth."

"But you told her we love *her* now, didn't you?"

Greg's silence made Tom pull his gaze from Savannah and look at him. "Tell me you made it clear that Beth was in the past but that our future lies with *her*. That we love her more than anything." His voice trembled.

Greg pursed his lips. "I might not have had the opportunity to say all that, exactly." He chanced a peep at Tom.

"For fuck's sake!" Tom scooted over to where Savannah stood. Opening his arms, he swept her into them and held her while she sobbed uncontrollably.

Greg joined them but didn't speak. He put his arm around her back and kissed the top of her head.

Tom's mind whirled with uncertainty and the revelations of the afternoon. He didn't know how long they stood there in silence, but a driver in a hurry suddenly beeped his horn at them, making them all jump.

"All right, I'm on it," Greg said, pulling the keys from his pocket.

"I'm parked up the street. I'll show you," Tom offered, steering Savannah toward the passenger door.

"I'm not coming," she murmured, pulling free of him and stepping onto the sidewalk.

Tom's heart sank. "What?"

"Come on. Move it!" The driver was getting fed up now.

"All right, all right," Greg snapped, climbing into his own driver's seat. "Don't move." He pointed at the others as Tom joined Savannah. His face was ashen as he drove away.

"Come on, beautiful. We need to talk," Tom said. "So much has happened today. We all need some time to figure everything out."

He tried to put his arms around her but she brushed him away. "Yeah, we do," she said.

His heart was in his mouth. "Savannah, we love you," he told her, praying she'd believe him.

They were both jostled as a crowd of shoppers barged past them.

"I need some time to myself," she said. "You're right, so much has happened."

"Are we moving too fast?" He put a hand on her shoulder, even more alarmed.

"I don't know. I don't know anything right now. It's like…as soon as something goes right, it all goes wrong again."

"But *we're* not wrong," he said. "Greg and I love you. You have to remember that. Nothing will ever change the way we feel about you."

She nodded as fresh tears began to trail down her face. "I have to go."

Tom held her shoulder a little tighter, glancing up the street for Greg. He turned back to her. "Go where? What do you mean, beautiful?"

"Home," she said.

He took a deep breath, his heart hammering. "Home as in *our* home? Bracken Ridge?"

She shook her head, dashing his hopes. "No. Upton Crossing."

"Why?"

"It's where I live. It's where all my things are. My clothes..." she indicated his attire that she was wearing. "I need my own stuff."

"Then we'll take you," he said. "It's no problem. I'll take you now. I'll just tell Greg..."

"No. I need to be on my own."

He stared at her in dismay. "Why?"

"I need some time to think properly, to get my bearings."

He swallowed hard, just as Greg ran up to them.

"There's a diner just up the road. How about some lunch? We missed out earlier." His cheerfulness quickly waned as he studied their faces.

"Don't you want to be with us?" Tom asked, ignoring him. He was still staring at Savannah.

"I just think we all need to take a step back," she said, shaking her head.

"From what? From us? From what we have? Last night?" Tom pleaded.

"Yes... No... Maybe."

Someone jostled her again and she huffed.

"We need to go somewhere to talk about this," Greg said. "Is this because of what I just did...or nearly did? Because of Beth?"

"Or because of my criminal record?" Tom added.

"Maybe all of it," she said, more tears cascading down her cheeks. "Look. I need to go home. I need to think about everything and work out where I stand."

"And what about us? Where do *we* stand?" Tom was feeling desperate. She was slipping out of their grasp and they'd only just gotten her.

"I don't know."

"With you?"

She shrugged.

"What the hell does that mean?" He was almost in tears himself.

"Hang on. Are you splitting up with us, sweetheart? Without talking things through? You just wanna walk away?" Greg looked stunned.

She shook her head. "I'm not saying that. I just want to go home and have some time on my own to think. That's all."

"Okay, we'll take you," Greg said.

"Don't you need to get Carla's truck back to her?" Tom asked.

"It can wait. We'll take you home and get you settled. Once we know you're okay, we can leave you there or you can grab some stuff or whatever and come back with us. Either to Mrs. H's or our place, your choice. Okay?" Greg was the voice of reason, and in that moment, Tom hated him for it.

"I can walk. That's how I —"

"Not an option. Come on. We'll take our truck. I'll figure Carla's out later." Greg wasn't taking no for an answer, much to Tom's relief, and they all marched along the road, despite Savannah's insistence that she could make her own way.

"I'll drive," Tom said, pulling out the keys. He was determined to take back some control, at least.

They all clambered in, Savannah in the middle, as usual.

Instead of cuddling into Greg's arm, she sat up straight, staring through the windshield with teary eyes.

"Say something," Greg told her after a few minutes of unbearable silence. Tom wasn't driving too fast, buying some time. "I did all the talking earlier, now I think it's your turn."

"I don't know what to say," she mumbled, still not looking at either of them.

"Are you mad at us?" Tom's stomach roiled as he asked her, afraid of the answer, and yet longing for something tangible to work with.

She shrugged.

Greg took a deep breath. "Okay. We loved Beth and now we love you. You're not her—nothing like her, in fact, but that might be what we love about you. You're you."

Her eyes didn't flicker.

"We're not a couple of violent thugs," Tom said, his voice quiet. "I just couldn't stand by and let that bastard insult Beth, just like Greg couldn't let Daniel get away with what he did to you. It wasn't a frenzied attack. It was trying to avenge an injustice."

"I know," she whispered, still not facing either of them.

"So you *don't* hate us?" Tom asked, holding his breath.

She slowly shook her head, turning to look up at him.

Tom stroked her flushed cheek. "Thank you."

She sniffed. "I just can't be with you now."

Chapter Eighteen

Savannah had a familiar sinking feeling in her gut as they pulled up outside the house at Upton Crossing. She tried to ignore it. It only added to the sickness roiling there, and the huge lump that had been stuck in her throat for the past couple of hours.

"Have you got a key?" Greg frowned.

She nodded. "Under the blue plant pot. It's always there."

The guys exchanged an uncertain look and she knew exactly what they were thinking. After moving his lover in and straightening up the garden, there was a good chance Daniel might have removed the spare key. She doubted it, though. Daniel was more likely to have forgotten it was even there. Besides, she knew the best window to force if she had to.

She shifted toward Greg, aware that neither of them had moved since the truck stopped.

Greg huffed, but she just gave him an expectant look and he slowly climbed out, holding his arms up to help her down. She loved how much care they took of her. She loved *them*.

His arms were warm and safe, and that familiar scent surrounded her as he lifted her to the ground. His lips came dangerously close to hers and her breath hitched.

"Looks like rain again. Let's get you inside," Tom said, coming around to their side of the truck.

Greg sighed and flung an arm around her as they made their way to the front door.

She'd been right about the key, and Greg got it as soon as they reached the step.

"Don't leave it there again," he told her, opening the door. "It's not safe."

She refrained from rolling her eyes. It was good of him to care about her, but she had to stand on her own two feet for once. The house was cold and smelled musty and damp. She remembered how unwelcoming it had always been. Daniel had forbidden her from putting cushions and throws around the place, and he detested the smell of fresh flowers or even potpourri.

"Will there be any food in here?" Tom asked, following them into the kitchen and looking around.

"I keep the freezer well stocked," she said, nodding. "I can look after myself, you know."

"I know," Tom said on a sigh. "But you don't have to. *We* want to look after you now." He took a step closer to her, but she stepped back, afraid that her new-found resolve might crumble at any moment.

"You don't have to worry," she said, shaking her head. "Daniel won't be back tonight, and I need some space."

"But it's cold and lonely out here and you haven't eaten all day. You shouldn't be on your own after everything that's happened. At least let us take you back to the bed-and-breakfast? You can spend the whole time up in your room if you want to, but at least there'll be someone there if you need them. And Mrs. H has both our numbers."

Greg seemed to have it all worked out, as usual.

"I told you. There's food in the freezer. I can light the fire. And I need some time to think. Please... After everything that's happened today, at least give me that much?"

Greg swallowed hard, his sad face clouding with realization. Tom sighed, as though finally resigning. They couldn't argue with her anymore.

"Shall we sit with you a while?" Tom asked.

She shook her head. "I just want to be on my own."

"Have you got a cell phone?" Greg asked, frowning.

"No, but there's a landline." She led them into the sitting room and pointed to a small table. "It's for emergencies only."

Greg tutted, but went over to where she indicated. "These are our numbers. Call anytime, even just to let us know you're okay." He jotted them down on a pad next to the old-fashioned phone.

She nodded.

"What's your number?" He asked, tearing off a page and handing it to her with a pencil.

She wrote it down without speaking.

"We'll call you later to make sure you're okay." He tucked it into his back pocket.

"There's no need. I—"

"And we'll come and get you in the morning, about half past seven." He wasn't listening to her protestations.

She stared at him.

"We can go for breakfast at the diner before we take you to work," he said. "I take it things went well with Sandy at the salon today?"

Savannah startled as she recalled that she hadn't gone back to her job this afternoon. With everything that had happened, she'd completely forgotten that she had work to do.

"I should've been there," she said, glancing at the wall clock. It was after five and the shop would be closing.

Greg shook his head, smiling. "Don't look so worried. Sandy probably knows all about what happened by now. You can't keep secrets in Cavern County."

Savannah recalled how all the ladies had been talking in the salon that morning. Everyone knew everything about everyone else. In a way, it would be a blessing not having to explain tomorrow, but on the other hand…

"So, they'll all be gossiping about me?" The knot twisted in her stomach.

Greg and Tom exchanged a look that reaffirmed her fears. Not only would they know that her husband was in jail but also what he'd done to her. She'd cringed when Tom had brought it up with Daniel in the first place but had been able to stay out of the way, hiding in a crowd of strangers. Tomorrow she wouldn't have that luxury.

Anger boiled inside her. If Tom hadn't rowed with Daniel, then no one would be any the wiser. *Why did he have to interfere?* She glared at him and he winced, as though reading her thoughts.

"I don't know what I'll be doing tomorrow, so it might be best if you don't come over," she told Greg.

He frowned. "But I thought you wanted that job?"

She shrugged, fighting the urge to yell at them both to get out of her house and never come back. "I did. I do. But I need to think it through. Thanks, anyway." She started walking back to the front door, hoping they'd follow suit. They didn't. *Damn.*

"You're mad at me. Aren't you, beautiful?" Tom stared at her defiantly.

"I think it would be better if you both left while we all process everything." She tried to sound reasonable, though a little voice inside her head was screaming, *yes, of course I am!*

Greg took a step toward her. "For what happened with Daniel or because Tom didn't tell you he had a criminal record?" He spoke slowly, as though trying to compute it all in his own mind.

"I'm guessing both." Tom sighed.

"Look… I think it's best if you guys go. Thanks for the ride and everything, but I really don't want to talk right now."

"Because you think we'll fight?" Tom asked.

Yes, of course we'll fucking fight! Savannah bit her lip. "I just think that things might be said in the heat of the moment that we could regret afterward."

"Regret? Like last night, you mean?" Tom looked horrified.

She swallowed hard.

Greg looked from Tom to Savannah, his face like stone. "Is that right, sweetheart? Do you regret last night? What we did? What we said to each other?"

Her face was hot and she fought back the tears. She could never regret what had happened between them. It had been perfect. It was just everything that happened this afternoon had marred a beautiful memory, and she couldn't stop blaming Tom. As for

Greg, she'd seen a completely different side to him, one that reminded her too much of the bully she'd just escaped from. This whole relationship was one step forward, two steps back, all the way.

She couldn't bear to look at their mortified expressions any longer, so she opened the front door, letting the cold air sweep in. "It's best you go now."

"Best for who? You? Because you'll be the only one getting any sleep tonight, beautiful," Tom bit at her. "We'll just be left dangling like a fish on a hook, waiting for you to decide which way we should jump. Is that what you want?" His eyes looked bigger than ever and his face was turning red.

Her stomach burned. She knew it didn't seem fair to either of them—and he sure was wrong about her getting any sleep—but his attitude annoyed her. She'd been trying to get them to leave so they wouldn't argue, but Tom seemed determined to have it out with her.

"Well, why don't you just go ahead and jump right off, then?" She barked the words at him, anger roiling inside her. "After all, it seems to me that you're quite happy to wade in and do whatever you please, regardless of how it affects anyone else."

"I did *not* wade in!" Tom snapped. "*He* was the one yelling at me in the damn street, not the other way around. He provoked a fight because he knew I'd hit someone before to defend a young woman and thought he could get me jailed again. But this time it didn't work. Well, not with *me*, anyway." He looked pointedly at Greg, who was seething.

"Yup, it was *my* turn to show what a good-for-nothing thug I am," Greg said, putting his hands up in submission. "And d'you know what? I'd do it again, too. Anything to show that fuckwad that we won't tolerate his shit." He took a step toward her, Tom following behind.

"I'm sorry if that means we're both a couple of punks, Savannah," Tom said, "but we just stand up for what we believe in, what we're passionate about. Sometimes that kind of fervor gets taken for a lack of self-control, but that's not how it's meant. We just can't stand by and watch such a massive injustice."

She stood back, allowing them to pass through the doorway. Relief was marred with sadness when she saw them standing on the doorstep in the dim light.

"Just or not, they won't keep him locked up forever," she said. "But when he's freed, it won't be *you* who's left to tolerate his shit."

She closed the door.

* * * *

"I can't believe we just left her there." Tom moaned as they pulled up behind Carla's truck. The roads around Almondine were much quieter than earlier, but there were still crowds piling into the bars and cafés.

"We didn't exactly get much choice, buddy," Greg reminded him. "Jeesh, don't these people have homes to go to?" He was waiting for a stream of pedestrians to clear so he could open his door.

"Maybe they don't wanna go home," Tom said.

Greg pursed his lips. "I know what you're saying, but you saw how it was. She'd tried to get us out before the fireworks, but you just wouldn't let it go, would you? You *had* to antagonize her."

"At least I got to the crux of the matter. If you'd had your way, we'd both be dangling on that hook, waiting for her to tell us which way to jump," Tom shouted, attracting the attention of some of the passers-by.

"Yeah, well, maybe I'd *rather* still be dangling." Greg's lips were tight as he spoke, much quieter than his buddy. "At least while I was on that hook, I still had a chance at happiness. Now, what've we got?"

He managed to open his door and walk over to Carla's truck. He climbed in and started the engine. Glancing at the seat beside him, he recalled how Savannah had looked just a few hours ago.

She'd been worried about Tom. Would Daniel seek him out and hurt him? Would he hit Daniel? Would history repeat itself? And what about Beth? He knew he hadn't said enough at the time to allay any fears she might have had about her. The guys were over her, but how could they convince Savannah of that? They should have tried harder. *He* should have made it clear from the start.

He spent the whole journey back to Pelican's Heath berating himself for the way he'd handled the entire situation. It was ironic that Savannah had assumed it was him who had the criminal record — then he almost did have. She'd been hurt and upset at the thought of him hitting someone, for whatever reason, then he'd gone right ahead and tried to do it in front of her, to her own husband. No wonder she'd asked them to leave tonight. She'd hit the nail squarely on the head when she'd talked about them doing things without worrying about who would be affected by them. And it was sad to hear that she was afraid of Daniel being freed and coming after her. Whatever else he did, he had to ensure that would never happen.

Dyson opened the door when he pulled up at the Shearer Ranch.

"Just returning Carla's pickup," Greg said, handing over the key.

"Great. You're back." Carla appeared behind the sheriff, in the hallway. "I've just taken some cookies out of the oven. Hope you're hungry."

Greg was happy to take her up on her offer and followed her into their warm kitchen. Matt was sitting at the table, drinking coffee. "Evening, boss."

"Sit down, Greg," Matt smiled at him while Dyson placed a warm drink in front of him.

"Ta-daa." Carla placed a cooling rack full of piping hot chocolate-chip cookies in the middle of the table, and she and Dyson sat down to join the others.

"Well, that husband of hers can sure cuss a blue streak," Dyson said, rolling his eyes. He took a cookie.

"Mind you, don't burn your hands," Carla warned with a smile. "Help yourself, Greg."

"Thanks." He smiled back at her. *She's a lot of fun, as well as being real pretty – though not as beautiful as Savannah.* "Actually, Dyson, I was hoping to ask you about him. He *will* go to prison for all this, won't he? I mean, what he did to Savannah, as well as all that false business stuff?"

"Well now, that all depends on the judge," Dyson said, with a thoughtful frown. "But I'd be surprised if he didn't get sent down, especially if Savannah testifies about his cruelty."

"Dyson told me what that fucker did," Carla said. "He can't be right in the head."

"Now, don't go adding any mental problems to the mix," Dyson warned her. "I'd hate to see him get off on a plea of diminished responsibility after what he did."

"I hadn't thought of that," Greg said, alarmed.

"Well, let's just hope *he* doesn't either. Mind you," Dyson went on, "he'd need all sorts of historical medical reports and stuff to go down that route and it's highly unlikely he'd have anything like that."

Greg gave a sigh of relief. "Savannah's afraid he'll come after her."

"Well, I suppose it could happen, no matter how long the sentence, but there'd be a lot of folks looking out for her once he got released, including the law enforcers. We're always on our guard for stuff like that."

"I'm sure he wouldn't get near her with you and Tom there to protect her, anyhow," Carla chirped up. "Where are they, by the way? Back at your house?"

Just then there was a crackle from Dyson's radio and he stood up and went to the other end of the kitchen to answer it.

"I'm not sure where Tom is. I presume he's gone home." Greg was a little embarrassed to admit they'd had a row, so he left that part out.

"And Savannah's with him?" Carla grinned knowingly.

"Well, not exactly…"

"I'm on my way," Dyson said into his radio, as he picked up his hat.

He frowned, looking back at Greg.

"There's a disturbance over at Upton Crossing."

Chapter Nineteen

Savannah dissolved in a heap of tears as soon as she locked the door on the two guys. She slid down the wall to wallow in the aftermath of her actions. *Why couldn't they have just left before things turned ugly?* There was no turning back from this now, which was exactly the situation she had strived so hard to avoid.

When their motor eventually started up, her heart lurched. The silence deafened her once they'd gone and she'd never felt so alone in her life.

It was getting dark in the little cottage and shadows haunted her where the drapes had been left open in some of the rooms, allowing the dusky light to filter in through the open doorways. She shuddered, not only because of the cold that surrounded her, consuming her, but also through fear. She was miles from anywhere. Alone.

Curling into a ball, she allowed the misery to pour out of her. She shut her eyes tight, burying her face in her arms while sadness engulfed her.

Savannah wasn't sure how long she'd sat on the hallway floor, but she must have fallen asleep at some point, as she opened her eyes to find the house in almost total darkness and a crick in her neck that hurt like the devil.

"This is stupid." Her own voice echoed, making her flinch.

She stood, stretching carefully. The first thing that hit her was the dank, musty smell of the old house. It certainly wasn't a home. She reached for the light, and the contrast made her eyes ache and water. Nevertheless, she went into the kitchen and switched that light on, too — and the one in the little utility and the lounge. She pulled the drapes, closing out the night, and switched on a radio for some company.

She forced herself to go into the bedroom, damping down memories of the last time she had stood here, with Tom waiting in the doorway. At the time, she'd thought she was right not to take any of her things back to Pelican's Heath. She hadn't wanted to cart the memories there with them. Now she saw that it was weakness. Facing up to those memories might have enabled her to exorcise them in some way — and would certainly have made dressing much more comfortable.

Pulling the curtains across, she shivered as her eye caught something moving near the railway track. It was too far away to make out its shape, and she hoped that the light from behind her had distorted its size, as it seemed quite large. A lot of the local wildlife had long since been scared off the railway, as the sound it made when a heavy-goods train was running could be quite deafening.

She went into the tiny bathroom and ran the shower while she undressed. There was no hurry, as it always took a while to heat up. Pulling a towel around her, she checked out her drawers for some clothes. They were empty, as was her half of the wardrobe. *I wonder if Belinda Hathaway had moved her things into my space.*

The cold air surrounded her, and she quickly went back into the bathroom and jumped under the shower. It wasn't as warm as she'd have preferred, but it was good to feel some heat on her weary body. She washed her hair as she considered her next move.

Despite not wanting to see the guys again just yet, she couldn't afford to let Sandy down, especially as she really wanted that job. She'd enjoyed female company this morning and had already made some lovely friends in Pelican's Heath. Without transport, though, it seemed like a hopeless pipedream.

Her mind wandered back to the handsome cowboys who had left her house tonight. They hadn't wanted to leave. That much had been plain. But how could she have a future with a couple of violent men? She had to admit they weren't cruel like Daniel, and she didn't really think they would hurt her, but it still didn't sit easy with her. Her heart wrenched at the thought of not seeing them again, though. They'd been so kind and caring with her — and they loved her. She had to admit to loving them, too, which just made the situation harder.

Tears were streaming down her cheeks, she realized, so she faced the showerhead, trying to wash away the hurt. It was going to take a lot more than water, that much was certain. Admitting defeat, she switched off the shower and grabbed the towel.

The bedroom was even colder when she went through, and she wished she'd found some clothes earlier and laid them out to be ready. She recalled

Belinda Hathaway mentioning something about some of her things being left in the old trunk, so she went over and cleared a pile of linen from the top before opening it.

Her hopes of finding something suitable to wear were dashed as soon as she saw the shredded material that lay there, and she couldn't stop fresh tears from flooding her face. Daniel had cut up all her best clothes, such as they were. The dress she'd gotten married in, the outfits she used to wear to church—on the occasions he would allow her to go—her party dress. Even her favorite nightgown was destroyed.

Feeling weak with sadness, she closed the lid and pulled the towel tighter around her shivering frame. She shouldn't have come back here.

A sudden noise startled her and she froze for a second. Someone was banging on the door. Her heart leaped. Tom and Greg? They were the only ones who knew she was here, the only people who might visit her at this time of night. They must have driven up while she was in the shower. She wondered if they'd been calling her, but, again, the sound of the water would have drowned out the ringtone.

Clutching the towel even tighter against her, she rushed out of the bedroom and up the hallway. Her anger with them dissipated in favor of relief that they were here. They still cared.

She turned the key then flung open the door and almost screamed with shock. It wasn't the handsome cowboys. It was an older man. She recognized him from the Shearer Ranch—Pete Bramhall, Daniel's partner.

"I saw the lights on," he said. "I thought I'd check on the place, make sure it wasn't being burgled or anything."

"It…it's not." She covered her chest with her arms, aware of his leering expression.

He frowned. "Now why would you wanna come all the way back here on your own?"

"I live here." She jutted out her chin. "Was there something you wanted, Mr. Bramhall?"

He looked surprised then he grinned. "Well, now you come to mention it…"

She immediately tried to shut the door but his foot jammed it open.

"You can't come in!" she yelled.

"I think you'll find I already have, darlin'." He lurched toward her, but she ran back into the living room and slammed the door shut before pulling a chair in front of it.

It didn't do much good, as Bramhall was a strong man, and he soon had it open, his hand grappling around the edge. It had bought her time to get to the phone, though.

"No, you don't!" There was a scraping sound as he tried to lever the door open farther.

With a scream, Savannah dropped the handset and grabbed a glass vase from a nearby shelf. She hit the back of his knuckles that were still clutching the side of the door. Part of the vase shattered against the wood, while he howled in agony. Without thinking, she thrust the vase against his flesh again, this time stabbing into his skin.

"Fucking bitch!" Anger seemed to make him stronger and he pushed the chair out of the way, enabling him to burst the door open. "You'll regret that!" he hollered as blood poured from his hand.

Savannah backed away, still holding the remains of the broken vase in one hand while she kept the towel wrapped tightly around her with the other. "You keep away from me," she warned him, trying to keep the tremor from her voice.

"Or *what*?" He sneered. "Face it, darlin'. You're nothing but a little whore. We both know you had something going with one of them cowboys back there, while you were still *married*, I might add."

Her blood boiled at the accusation.

"Well now, they obviously didn't want you or you wouldn't be here now, would ya?" He was clearly enjoying upsetting her.

"It's none of your damn business!" she snapped.

"Well, see, that's exactly where you're wrong, darlin'. 'Cause you just wrecked *my* business, along with that stupid bastard husband of yours, so the way I see it, you owe me." He took another step closer to her, and she waved the vase in front of him, in what she hoped was a menacing fashion.

"I don't owe you anything!"

"Oh yes, you do. And I'm gonna take it, starting with you." He grabbed for her with a filthy hand and she tried to step backward but was met with the wall. She yelped, and he wrenched the vase from her hand. While she tried to push him away, he leaned in, pinning her to the exposed bricks with his injured hand on her midriff, heaving his weight against her.

"No!" she screamed.

"You want me to use this on that pretty face of yours, or are you going to give me what I want?" His voice was like gravel, and he spat as he spoke, his rancid breath making her almost as sick as his words.

She shook her head in horror and disbelief. "No."

"Well, we'll see about that, shall we?" He raised the vase backward.

"You heard the lady," a familiar voice growled, as Tom grabbed his arm and twisted it right up his back until the vase smashed to the floor. "She said no."

"Bastard!" Bramhall roared with fury and pain, but Tom just used that arm as a lever to yank him backward, thus pulling him off Savannah.

Her whole body shook as she slid out of his reach, and she hugged the towel closer to her frame. Tom then slammed Bramhall into the brick wall, eliciting a feral howl from the fucker.

"Hand me that phone cable," Tom called to her. "We'll use it to tie him up."

Savannah rushed over to the phone, grabbing the handset off the floor. She heard a cracking sound and was mortified to see that Bramhall had jolted his head back sharply, head-butting Tom, who fell backward, just giving his nemesis time to kick him to the floor.

"Tom!" she screamed as blood trickled down his face. He looked dazed for a second then tried to grab Bramhall, but he wasn't fast enough.

There was a glint of silver as the fucker pulled a knife out of his boot and flailed it through the air with a sickening guffaw. From his position on the floor, Tom quickly slid his foot along, swiping Bramhall off his feet. As he tumbled headfirst to the floor, his face bashed into the little telephone table.

Savannah wrapped the phone cord around his neck while Tom grabbed the knife from his hand.

"You won't get away with this…"

Savannah pulled the cord tighter, cutting off his words — as well as his air supply. She loosened it again. "Keep your mouth shut!" she warned him, adrenalin pumping through her veins like a steam train.

"I'd do as the lady says, if I were you." Tom held up the knife, panting hard.

"That's good advice."

They all looked up to see Dyson pointing a gun at Bramhall, who scowled furiously.

Greg and Carla appeared from behind the sheriff, closely followed by Matt, who took the cuffs from his brother and went over to Bramhall.

"He broke my damn arm," the prisoner protested.

"I wouldn't cuss in the lady's house if I were you," Matt said, yanking both Bramhall's arms behind his back, despite his yelling. "Especially as she's still holding that phone cord."

Savannah immediately dropped the cable, her vision blurred by more tears.

Matt frog-marched Bramhall outside while Carla pulled off her coat and wrapped it around Savannah, who was shivering uncontrollably.

"If you still wanna stay here tonight, we're staying with you," Greg said, throwing an arm around her.

Savannah shook her head.

"No arguments," Greg said.

"I don't want to stay here," she clarified.

"Hallelujah for that." He squeezed her, but she was still concerned about Tom. "He'll be fine," Greg added, clearly reading her mind. "Hopefully it knocked some sense into his skull."

"Thanks for your concern there, bro." Tom grinned.

"We'll take him in and leave you guys to it," Dyson said, having left Matt in the truck with their prisoner.

Carla gave Savannah a quick hug and kissed her cheek. "Y'all get some rest now, ya hear? Matt won't be expecting you too early in the morning. Just come when you're ready. And you might wanna get him checked out first." She nodded toward Tom.

"We will. Thanks, Carla." Greg gave her a friendly hug and she followed Dyson out the door.

"Are you sure you're okay?" Savannah frowned at Tom, who had pulled out a handkerchief to wipe up the blood that trickled down his cheek.

"Yeah, I'm fine." He smiled at her. "Are you coming back to our house, or…?"

"Yes, please."

Both her men enveloped her in a gentle hug that neither seemed to want to end. The front door was still wide open and a gust of wintery night air reminded them all where they were.

"Do you want to get your stuff?" Greg asked her, as they peeled their bodies from one another.

Savannah looked down at the towel she was wearing with a grimace. "There's nothing left to take. But I'd better get some clothes on."

Greg grinned as Tom went to shut the front door.

She quickly went back to the bedroom and put on Tom's clothes again. A thought suddenly struck her, and she yanked over a small rug that hid a wonky floorboard. After snaking her hand inside, she pulled out a small shiny bracelet. The silver looked tarnished, but she could just read her name etched in script across the front of it. She'd had it since she had been a little girl and it was the only reminder of her childhood, the last time in her life that she'd been truly happy. She stuffed it into her pocket. Her heart was hammering and she couldn't wait to be out of there.

"Take that key with you this time," Greg told her as they left the house

Savannah did as he'd said.

"I'll drive," Greg insisted before they all clambered into the pickup.

For once, Tom didn't argue.

Chapter Twenty

"You sure you want to come back to our house? We'll take you to the bed-and-breakfast if you'd rather?" Greg offered as they reached a turn in the road.

"Quite sure," Savannah told him with a nod. "Besides, Mrs. Hodges'll be fast asleep by now. Have you seen how late it is?"

Greg nodded and took the back road for Bracken Ridge.

Savannah snuggled even closer into Tom's side. His arm was draped around her shoulder, holding her like he was never going to let her go.

"Are you okay?" She gazed up at him. "We need to get you checked out, don't forget."

"I'm fine." Tom's voice was as soft as his smile.

"Matt won't let you work tomorrow until you've seen the doc," Greg reminded him.

"Yeah, but it's a bit late now, don't you think? I'll drop by the clinic tomorrow."

"I'll make sure you do." Greg sounded adamant.

"I was only stunned for a second. I didn't black out or anything," Tom insisted.

"Even so, you hit your head. You know what that means." Greg parked outside the house.

Savannah frowned. "What does it mean?" Her concern level rose.

"It means he's not allowed to go sleep for a while," Greg told her, matter-of-factly. "Come on. Let's get inside."

"I thought that was an old wives' tale," Savannah queried as she clambered out after Tom.

Both guys used the lights on their cell phones to guide them inside, as it was pitch black out in the country lane.

"Really?" Tom looked disappointed as he switched on the hall light and they all went in.

"I don't think it's worth taking any chances," Greg said with a grin. "We should figure out a way of keeping him awake, I reckon."

A warmth traveled through Savannah's body as she caught the glint in Greg's eye and realized what he was suggesting. Her heart beat a little quicker at the thought of all the ways in which they could ensure that Tom didn't fall asleep for an hour or so.

"You're right. We mustn't risk Tom's health just for the sake of a couple of hours of sleep," she said, nodding.

The guys chuckled as they all took off their coats and boots and left them on a large box in the hallway.

"But first, you need to eat," Tom said, steering Savannah in the direction of the kitchen. "You missed your lunch today, and I'm guessing you didn't have anything when you got to your house, either, did you?"

Savannah shook her head.

"That's what I thought." Tom opened the refrigerator and pulled out a large meatloaf. "We haven't got much in, I'm afraid, but I managed to pick this up earlier, so I hope you like it?"

"Thank you," Savannah salivated at the sight. She was touched that he had noted that she hadn't eaten since breakfast and was flattered that, although they didn't have much food in the house, they were willing to share what they had.

Greg grabbed a large bag of potato chips from a cupboard as Tom sliced the loaf.

"I hope *you're* not planning on having any of that," Greg told him.

Tom frowned. "What? Why? You know I love meatloaf."

Greg shook his head, taking the plate from him. "You bashed your head, remember? It's best not to eat for a while after something like that. Come on, Savannah. We'll take this upstairs."

Savannah noticed Greg's smirk before she followed him upstairs, recalling that there was nowhere to sit in the living room. Tom huffed but brought up the rear.

The bedroom was warm and welcoming. Greg put the food on the side table and plated some for her while she sat on the bed.

"Thank you." She couldn't help feeling guilty that Tom wasn't allowed any as she tucked into the meatloaf. "This is delicious."

"I'll go take a shower," Tom said, gazing longingly at the food. He turned and went into the en suite bathroom.

"Are you *sure* he's not allowed to eat?" Savannah asked Greg once the water was running in the next room.

"We should err on the side of caution," Greg said with a wink as he reached over and took another slice for himself. "You can't be too careful with a head injury."

Savannah rolled her eyes but ate her supper. It was clear the guys were making more out of Tom's injury than was necessary, but she liked the idea of keeping him awake for a while — especially in this huge bed.

They'd finished eating by the time Tom returned from the bathroom. His hair looked black as it dripped down his neck, and the thin stubble on his face seemed to glisten in the lamplight. He looked quite relaxed, with a small towel around his waist and a big smile.

She licked her lips — and not because of the meatloaf. He looked edible and she blushed at the thought of having him for dessert.

Greg stood then took the plate from her to return it to the table.

Savannah's heart hammered and her breath began to pant as both guys sat on the bed on either side of her.

"Savannah, we don't mean to pressure you in any way," Tom told her. "If you want to just hang out here a while — we can sleep in a different room, if you prefer — while all this settles down, you're more than welcome. We're not making any assumptions or demands on you by inviting you to stay."

"I want to be here with you guys," she told him.

Greg tucked a finger under her chin and turned her to look at him. "You realize you're quite safe now, don't you? Neither your husband nor that Bramhall guy can get to you. Dyson said he's got enough evidence to keep them locked up for a very long time. And, of course, while he's in jail, Daniel can't contest your divorce — if you want one, that is." His eyes widened a little as he looked at her questioningly.

"Yes, of course I do." She gulped, looking from one to the other. "Look. I'm really sorry about what happened. I was just afraid that…"

"It's okay. We know." Tom put a hand up to reassure her. "I should've told you before about my past. It's just that I was afraid that after all you'd gone through with Daniel, you might think—"

"I had no right thinking anything," she said, cutting him off. "I jumped to the wrong conclusions. You guys only wade in when it's really important to you. You're not mindless thugs. Christ, look at me with that phone cable. I could've killed that fuckwad. I almost did because I was so riled up. Now I know how you guys felt."

"And yet you're not a violent person. It's just circumstances that make you do things like that on the spur of the moment." Greg smiled at her.

"That, and the damn injustice of what people do to you and your loved ones," Tom added, stroking her arm.

She turned and gazed into his deep, dark eyes. So much emotion oozed from them, so much…

"I love you guys," she whispered.

They both put their arms around her in a tender hold. Tom's naked chest pressed against her and she inhaled his gorgeous scent as she buried her head in his shoulder. Greg nestled in behind her, smothering her in his warmth and affection.

Slowly she lifted her face toward Tom's. His eyes were shining and his lips were parted. She reached up and pressed her mouth against his. He opened it and his soft tongue probed her mouth.

He held her a little tighter and the bed dipped as Greg moved. Tom ran his fingers through her hair while he stroked her back. She groaned from deep within her as she glowed hot with need, and their kiss became deeper and more passionate.

Savannah's nipples were hard, penetrating the cotton shirt. A sudden gush escaped her pussy and she gasped, aware that she was still wearing borrowed clothes. She didn't have time to waste on her embarrassment, though, as Greg returned to the bed, his hot body closing in behind her again.

She slowly drew back from Tom and opened her eyes, turning to acknowledge Greg. It was then that she noticed he was now stark naked. The smoldering expression in his eyes told her she soon would be too, and her breath hitched with excitement.

Sure enough, while he took her lips in a lingering kiss, Greg found her shirt buttons, which he swiftly undid. Tom pulled the shirt from her body, making her nipples jut out even more while her whole body tingled.

The guys were adept at teamwork, as Tom pulled her back against him, so she was now lying on top of him, her back to his warm chest. Greg made short work of removing her jeans.

"You sure about this, baby?" Tom murmured in her ear, roaming his big hands over her breasts and down her torso.

She could hardly speak with anticipation. "Oh yes," she assured them in a rasping whisper.

Greg carefully held her legs apart and inhaled the scent of her pussy. Then he delved his tongue into her folds, exposing her to the cool air. It was exquisite. Her body was flushed inside and out, and the contrast of the guy's hot bodies and the cooler air that surrounded them all was lush.

Tom pinched her nipples, eliciting yelps and groans from her as the tiny pain bloomed into inexplicable pleasure. She was excited and aroused as he caressed up and down her body, sometimes stroking her, sometimes grazing his nails against her skin. He nuzzled into her neck, bending down to kiss and lick at her tingling flesh.

Greg lapped at her juices and swept from her back hole to her aching clit in long, smooth motions that sent judders ricocheting through her.

"Scream as loud as you want. We don't have any neighbors to disturb." Tom's voice was low and rough as gravel as he urged her on.

Savannah hadn't thought about neighbors. Her mind had turned to the most delicious mush and she couldn't think of anything except these two gorgeous hunks and the pleasure they were bringing her.

She grabbed at the bed cover and wrung it between her fingers. Her eyes were partially closed as she savored every sensation they bestowed on her. The whole room was filled with grunts and moans, muttered words and deep gasps.

Passion like she had never experienced in her life rose through Savannah's body. Just when she thought the feeling couldn't get any better, it did. With yelps and cries of ecstasy, she tipped her head back, lolling from side to side as emotion and pleasure overtook her.

Greg ran his tongue right along her perineum, culminating in a huge swipe over her clit while Tom pinched hard on both her nipples. Her screams filled the air as tears rolled down her cheeks.

Through the haze of her need, she heard the guys murmuring to her, but she was incapable of answering them. Bright colors and lights like fireflies filled her blurry vision. She panted for air while clawing at the coverlet.

Tom peppered tiny kisses all over her head, while Greg licked at her juices and her inner thighs.

Eventually she began to float back to earth and she opened her eyes to see Tom smiling down at her.

"You okay, sweetheart?"

She nodded and looked down to see Greg grinning up at her from his position between her legs. He seemed to have taken root down there — and she wasn't complaining.

Something hard jabbed into her back, reminding her that these guys weren't unaffected by the events of the evening, and she imagined their erections must be getting quite painful by now.

Tom helped her sit up while Greg steadied her as she crawled off his buddy's body and sat on the soft coverlet.

"That was...amazing," she told them, still trying to catch her breath.

"I'd agree with that," Greg told her, beaming. He stood up and stretched himself, straightening out his back.

"Are you okay?" She guessed he must be quite uncomfortable.

"Don't worry about me. I couldn't be better."

She looked quizzically at Greg, who then made himself comfy taking Tom's place on the bed. Her anticipation rose. She wasn't quite sure what they had in mind, but she *was* sure she was about to enjoy it. The expressions on their faces told her that much.

"Wanna get on top?" Greg murmured, winking at her.

Her breath hitched. "Are you going to make love to me again?" Not that she was complaining—far from it—but she had rather assumed that it would be Tom's turn by now.

"Yup. If that's okay with you?" Greg grinned.

Savannah's insides heated even more.

"So am I," Tom murmured into her ear.

She gaped at him.

"I'm more of a back-door kind of guy, if you catch my drift?" Tom's deep voice made her pussy clench—almost as much as his words.

"You ever had it back there, sweetheart?" Greg asked her.

She shook her head, excitement and anticipation taking her breath away.

"That's what we thought. Which is partly why I've got that pleasure—providing you want to, of course?" Tom's eyes were bigger and darker than ever as he gazed at her.

She swallowed hard. Daniel would never have entertained any such idea, not that she would have wanted him to. She'd read about anal sex in books—the sort of books that she kept well-hidden from her husband—but assumed it would be painful, although the idea of it excited the hell out of her. Somehow, she knew Tom would be gentle with her, though, and her stomach lurched with excitement at the thought.

"The other reason why Tom gets to go first is that his cock's much smaller than mine. You could be quite sore if I tried, especially for your first time." Greg burst out laughing while reaching into a drawer on the nightstand. He handed a tube of ointment and a condom to Tom.

"Very funny, Tom replied, shaking his head. He held the cream up to show Savannah. "We've got plenty of lube, baby. No one's going to hurt you if we can possibly avoid it."

She nodded. "I'd love to try," she whispered, blushing.

"We'll take it slowly and you can stop anytime you want. You just have to say the word," Tom assured her with a brilliant smile. He leaned forward and gave her a lingering kiss. Heat extended right down to her pussy, which was getting wetter by the second.

Greg cleared his throat, eliciting a chuckle from Tom, who slowly freed her mouth.

"Getting a little uncomfortable back here," Greg remarked.

Savannah looked over and noticed the size of Greg's erection. "No wonder," she said, her eyes wide.

Greg grinned before applying a condom.

"Bragging, as always." Tom shook his head with a snigger. "Come on." He helped her straddle Greg, running his hands down her arms as she got comfortable.

"You go as slowly as you'd like, baby," Tom said as she hovered over the top of Greg's enormous cock.

"Thanks for that, buddy," Greg moaned.

Savannah giggled. "What about you?" she asked Tom.

"Oh, don't worry about me." He smiled. "I'll be right behind you."

Greg took hold of her hands while Tom relinquished his grip on her to get into position.

"You sure about this, sweetheart?" Greg checked, his voice as soft as velvet.

"Yup." She'd never been surer.

"You're in charge," he said with a nod.

She squeezed his hands hard as she slowly impaled herself onto his weeping cock. It was hard as a rock, although the skin was satiny soft. Given its enormity, she was surprised that it didn't hurt her as she gradually made her way down his length. Once she reached its base, Greg let go of her and placed his hands around her waist.

Reaching out, she ran her fingers over his smooth chest. He looked so gorgeous lying there, waiting patiently for her next move. She gazed into his blue eyes that were fixed on her.

Slowly she raised back up his shaft, as he helped support her. She was almost at the tip when she began her next descent. Greg helped her raise and lower her body over and over, stimulating different nerve endings with each movement. His thumbs brushed her folds, almost touching the tip of her clit before retreating again, leaving her on the edge of what she knew would be the most magnificent orgasm.

Tom roamed his hands up and down her back and shoulders, occasionally slipping under her arms to fondle her heaving breasts.

She closed her eyes and moaned with elation as both guys murmured to her and stroked her. Feeling almost dizzy with anticipation, she jumped as Greg swiped over her hard nub and she opened her eyes wide and screamed her release into the night. Her pussy felt as if it were boiling over and the next minute it seemed to expand even more as Greg's erection became bigger and he roared like a feral beast as he exploded into the thin rubber.

They were both still gasping for breath when Tom sprang into action.

"Bend forward, baby," he murmured from behind her.

She did as he said, her head still filled with the wonder of her orgasm — and Greg's.

Although Greg's cock must have shrunk a little, it still seemed huge inside her, and she was surprised to find it not falling out as Daniel's always did as soon as he'd come. Greg's was still touching her sensitive nerves, making her shudder with delight.

"Right over." Tom's voice was rasping now, and she guessed he wasn't far from his own release.

The air around them was thick with their body heat and the scent of sex. It all added to her excitement and, she guessed, theirs. She leaned forward even more and was thrilled when Greg took the opportunity of taking her mouth in a lingering kiss. Her breasts were squashed against his chest and she ran her hands though his hair.

"That's it, baby. You've got it," Tom said a little louder, his voice gaining an edge as he clearly fought to keep his restraint.

The thought of Tom feeling uncontrollable delighted Savannah even more, and she moaned into Greg's mouth.

Slowly, Tom fed his cock — which didn't feel any smaller than Greg's — into her ass, while pulling her cheeks wide open. Savannah gulped and dug her knees into the mattress, spreading her legs as far as she could. She had expected to feel more pain, but it was just a little uncomfortable for a few seconds as she stretched to accommodate Tom's girth. The sensation was like nothing on earth. It was strange but oddly exhilarating.

Tom's body was wrapped over hers, although his weight was off her. She didn't have time to work out how he was managing to control it, as he thrust in and out of her more and more rapidly, awakening nerves she hadn't even known existed. She had to pull away from Greg's mouth to enable herself to breathe, as she hitched her breath and gasped in wonder at the strange but wonderful sensations bombarding her.

She was full to the brim, with Tom's cock in her ass while Greg's was still in her pussy, and it didn't take long for the guys to fall into a teeter-totter motion, with one filling her while the other retreated, then vice versa.

It felt amazing and she made all manner of groans and cries as more passion than she thought possible rose inside her. The guys moaned and growled as their excitement matched hers, and suddenly, there was a deafening yell as all three of them climaxed together.

She was stretched beyond belief as the guys' cocks engorged for the final time, and they filled the little rubber sacks, expanding them — and her — even farther. She had no pain, just insurmountable pleasure, as her orgasm swept through her whole body like a tsunami, riding the wave of their passion.

Moments later, Tom slid out of her and moved off her, before gently lifting her onto the bed next to Greg.

The guys left the room as her eyes fell shut against the soft pillow. She guessed they must be desperate to take those condoms off and get cleaned up, and she supposed she'd need to get herself washed as soon as they'd finished in the bathroom but instead, she fell asleep.

* * * *

When she awoke, the guys were holding her and the birds were singing outside. Sunlight and the smell of fresh coffee greeted her.

"Good morning, beautiful," Tom said, with a smile.

She wiped a hand over her face. "Morning." She couldn't stop the shit-eating grin that spread across her face. She was a little sore but deliriously happy after the previous night.

She looked over to Greg and was surprised that he appeared wide awake, too.

"Did you guys get any sleep last night?" she asked with a giggle.

They exchanged a look that set alarm bells ringing in her ears. "What?" Her eyes darted from one to the other.

"Want some coffee?" Greg offered, passing her over a mug.

"No, I want to know what's wrong."

The sickly feeling in her gut suddenly erased all the joy she had enjoyed on waking. The way the guys kept looking at each other quashed all her excitement and she was left with a feeling of dread.

"Okay." Greg put the drink back on the nightstand.

She held up a finger. "Do you mind if I go take a shower before we talk? I won't be a minute."

"Sure," Tom replied, "take your time. There's a spare toothbrush on the side, too."

She tried to cover her body with her hands as she hurried over to the bathroom. She didn't think it would matter if they saw her not-so-perfect frame after last night, but somehow it did right now.

The water was warm and soothed her aching muscles. Her thoughts drifted back to the previous night and the fun she'd had with those guys. The thought that they might have been disappointed in her hurt like the devil. Maybe they just wanted a one-night stand? Tears streamed her face at the idea, and she lifted her eyes to the oncoming torrent to wash them away.

She had been so sure last night that they were sincere, that this was what they wanted. That *she* was what they wanted. Could it be that in the cold light of day they'd had second thoughts? Or had they been stringing her along from the start? Somehow, she couldn't believe that—or, at least, she didn't *want* to believe it.

After wrapping a towel around her, she stepped out of the shower and cleaned her teeth. At least if they were going to have a showdown, she would feel a little better being clean. A comb lay by the washbasin and she borrowed it to try to tame her hair. It wasn't behaving as well as she'd have liked, but it would have to do. Taking a deep breath, she went back into the bedroom.

The guys were already dressed, and she felt a little nervous in just her towel.

Greg was staring out the window, while Tom sat on the edge of the bed.

"Guys, it's okay. I get that you've changed your minds about me," she began, somehow feeling that if she led the conversation, she could cope better. "It's okay, really."

"What?" Greg darted around, frowning.

"Baby, you've got this wrong. Come and sit down. We need to explain." Tom patted the space next to him on the bed.

She swallowed hard. If she got physically close to these guys, all her resolve would disappear and she'd end up a crying wreck. She couldn't allow that to happen. Not now.

"I don't need an explanation." She jutted out her chin, standing her ground. "It's perfectly fine that you've had second thoughts about me."

"It is not—and we haven't," Greg insisted.

It was her turn to frown as her gaze flitted from him to Tom.

"Savannah, last night was incredible," Tom said. "We want you to move in with us. Stay with us. Marry us. Have kids with us." He looked wary as he spoke.

Her insides melted. "What?" It was too much to believe.

"Only if you want to," Greg added, studying her expression.

"Yes," she could hardly speak. "But…"

"We know you're already married," Tom said.

She shrugged. "I don't feel married. And besides, like I said last night, I want to get divorced from Daniel. He never loved me. Not like—"

"Like us," they finished for her, speaking in unison.

She smiled, relaxing a little more.

"Yes. And you did say that with Daniel locked away, I should get the divorce without any problems, didn't you?" She gazed up at Greg, who had come to stand closer to her now.

"That's right. That's what Dyson said, and he should know."

"Great. Not that there's any rush or anything," she said, pursing her lips. She was a little concerned that they might think she was too eager.

The two men exchanged one of those looks again, the kind that made her nervous and dread what was coming next.

"Okay." She marched over and plunked herself on the bed next to Tom. Greg followed and sat on the other side of her. She liked being sandwiched between these cowboys. "Which one of you is going to tell me what's wrong?"

"Looks like we're busted, bro," Tom said, raising his eyebrows at Greg.

"Sweetheart, how do you really feel about marriage and kids—the whole shebang?" Greg asked her.

She stared into his big blue eyes. "I'd love it," she told him. "It's what I've always wanted. Only…I shouldn't have married Daniel."

"Then why did you?" Tom asked.

She turned to face him, her face flushing. "I was pregnant. I was happy about it. I thought it was what we both wanted, anyway. We got married but then I had a miscarriage." She was determined not to cry as she explained, but the pity on Tom's face was almost too much to bear. "I was heartbroken, but Daniel was horrid about it. He said I'd tricked him into marriage."

"I thought I hated him before, but I've just realized just how much I despise that fucker," Greg growled from behind her.

"I didn't only marry him for the baby," she said, turning to face him. "I thought we loved each other. I soon realized how wrong I was about that. I wish I'd never married him, but what could I do? He didn't want me, but he refused to get a divorce."

"He didn't deserve you," Tom told her, putting a warm hand on her arm.

That small touch, that tiny gesture, was enough to open the floodgates, and all the hurt and upset came tumbling to the fore as tears cascaded down her flushed cheeks. Both guys threw their arms around her, holding her while she sobbed.

"I thought you'd changed your minds about me," she whispered, when the guys finally finished kissing every tear away.

Greg stood and fetched the box of tissues from the nightstand, then he crouched down in front of her. "Never." He gave a self-deprecating smile. "Sweetheart, there's something I need to tell you, though."

She sniffed hard, wiping her face. It was easier to look at them both at once with him in this position, but she wasn't sure she wanted to face them both right then. Taking a deep breath, she braced herself.

"I think you'd better just come out with it, Greg," she said after a lengthy pause. "Right now, I'm imagining all sorts of things and not one of them is good."

He cleared his throat. "Okay. Last night — which was fantastic, by the way…"

"I know," she agreed.

"Good." He looked thoughtful. "You're not on the pill, are you?"

She frowned then the penny dropped. She went numb for a second. "No, why? You both used condoms, remember?"

She stared at their guilty faces, her heart pumping like a bass drum.

"Mine broke," Greg said sheepishly. "It was my fault. I should have changed it after my first orgasm, but I got caught up in the moment and just kept going. It must have weakened and it tore."

"It was my fault, actually," Tom said. "If I hadn't been so keen to get going right after you guys had come, you'd have had time to change it for a new one. I guess I was a little too eager."

Savannah took a moment to compute their words. "So, I could be pregnant?" Butterflies held a rave in her stomach.

Greg bit his lip. "Yep." His eyes became wider as he was clearly trying to fathom how she felt about it. She was trying to figure it out, too.

"Are you mad at us, beautiful?" Tom asked.

She gaped at him. "Mad? No."

Tom narrowed his eyes, studying her face. "We want to marry you, not just because of this. Whether you're carrying our baby or not, it's what we want."

She nodded.

"It just might be a little sooner than we expected," Greg said, watching her face for a reaction.

"We don't have to. Even if I am, it doesn't mean —"

"We're not like him," Greg bit back.

Tom threw him an angry look. "What he means is —"

"I know. You're nothing like Daniel. And I'd love to marry you, whether I'm pregnant or not," she said.

"Really? So, you're sure you're not angry?" Greg's face lit up as he relaxed.

"Why would I be? I'd love to get pregnant with you guys. If not sooner, then how about later?" She shrugged as a warmth spread through her stomach.

"Yes. Of course. I mean... Oh, God, I love you, Savannah." Greg threw his arms around her and held her close.

"What he said," Tom murmured in her ear as he, too, held her tight.

"I love you guys," she whispered, trying to catch her breath in all the excitement. A thought occurred to her. "Hang on. Aren't you supposed to be working today?" She pulled back a little and they released her.

"I rang Matt earlier and explained the situation," Greg said. "We may pop over later, but he said we're due some time off, anyway."

She nodded. "I should check with Sandy to see if I still have a job. I can't believe I abandoned her yesterday."

"She'll understand," Tom assured her. "Folks around here are very accommodating, you know?"

"I thought we might do some shopping," Greg piped up. "You could use some clothes, we need to get some food and maybe we could look at some furniture — unless we're planning to live in this bedroom, not wear clothes and snack on junk forever more."

Savannah smiled. "Now, there's an idea."

Tom flashed his dark eyes at her enticingly. "Well, if Greg hasn't managed to get you pregnant with his broken condom, we could always try it the conventional way," he murmured, holding her a little tighter.

She licked her lips as Greg sat back on the bed and stroked her neck, sending shivers down her back. "I like the sound of that," she whispered.

Want to see more from this author? Here's a taster for you to enjoy!

The Cowboys of Cavern County: Two for Trinity
Bella Settarra

Excerpt

"Hey-oll—you didn't tell us she was *that* cute!" Jarrod whistled as the petite, pink-haired girl climbed down from the train.

"Behave," Frank murmured under his breath as they walked toward her. "Remember what I told you."

Cordell rolled his eyes at his buddy, shaking his head in disbelief, but said nothing. *Trust Jarrod...* He gazed over at the girl and had to admit she was beautiful.

"Trinity, my, how you've grown." Sylvia was the first to approach the elfin girl, and the hug she gave her niece looked like it might snap her right in two.

"Aunt Sylvia, it's so nice to see you again." Trinity smiled, although her eyes maintained a melancholy expression. "And Uncle Frank, how good of you to fetch me. I was expecting to call a cab. How's your arm?" She frowned as she studied his left arm, encased in a sling across his chest.

Frank stood forward and gave her a hug, too. "It's fine, sugar. Don't you worry about that. I just fell a little awkwardly, the doctor said. Dang horse got spooked by a mouse or something and reared up suddenly. I didn't realize what was happening until I hit the ground." He chuckled. "Still, like I always say, where there's no sense, there's no feeling." He tipped his head as he let her go. "This here's Jarrod and Cordell." He gestured toward the two guys who stepped forward to join them.

Cordell watched Jarrod smile broadly at the pretty waif and cringed inside, unsure of how she would react to them. To his surprise, she held out her hand.

"Pleased to meet you. I'm Trinity Ellis," she said.

Jarrod seemed a little bemused as he shook her hand, though he was still smiling. "Jarrod Parker. Good to meet you, darlin'."

Cordell noticed her blush slightly before she turned to him, holding that hand out again.

"Hi Trinity, I'm Cordell Bray." He took her tiny hand in his, surprised that such a little woman had such a firm shake. She wore bright pink nail varnish that matched her hair, and her palm was warm and soft against his skin. He couldn't resist prolonging their shake a little as he continued, "Welcome to Cavern County."

She gave him a shy smile before withdrawing it. "Thank you."

"We came to carry your bags—and to do the driving, of course," Jarrod told her, glancing around.

"Oh, that's very kind. But I've only got this." She had a yellow, oversized handbag she was clinging to for dear life. "Everything else is gone." Tears filled her big, green eyes as she said it, and Cordell's heart went out to her.

"Well, let's get you home and settled in," Sylvia offered quickly, throwing an arm around Trinity and leading her toward the car. "I'll bet you haven't eaten in a while, have you?"

Cordell hung back a little as Frank followed the women.

"Looks like she hasn't eaten in a month of Sundays," Jarrod whispered, getting closer to his friend.

"Shh." Cordell rolled his eyes again. Jarrod was a lovely guy, but tact had never been his strong point.

"I'm only saying," Jarrod said, holding his hands up in surrender. "She seems like she'll get blown away if the wind springs up."

"Cut it out," Cordell murmured. "You know dang well she's been through hell and back. The last thing she needs is your smart-ass comments. And don't think I didn't notice you giving her the eye, either. She's off limits, remember?"

"She's still beautiful. You can't deny that," Jarrod muttered with his sing-song tone. "I saw the way you gawked at her, bro. You can't tell me you don't fancy her."

"That's not the point. Just cut it out, will you?" Cordell was muttering through clenched teeth as they neared the car.

Jarrod grinned.

Cordell sighed.

"Stop worrying," Jarrod whispered into his ear before disappearing around the other side of the car.

Cordell couldn't help smiling as he climbed into the driver's seat. Nothing fazed Jarrod. That was one of the many things he liked about his best friend.

"I've got the guest room all ready for you," Sylvia was telling Trinity as they drove toward Pelican's Heath.

"That's very nice of you," Trinity replied, in a small voice. She was sitting in between her uncle and aunt, who seemed to dwarf her, although they weren't exactly large people.

Cordell watched her through his rear-view mirror. She looked bewildered and he realized she must still be in shock after what had happened. "Do you like to ride, Trinity?" he asked, trying to keep the conversation light.

"Yes, I used to," she told the back of his head. "I haven't ridden for quite a while, though. Think I might be a bit rusty by now." Her voice sounded a little more cheerful, and he noticed in the rear-view mirror how she flushed slightly.

"Well, you'll get plenty of opportunity in Pelican's Heath," Jarrod offered. "Although I'd advise you to stay on the horse. Your uncle's method of riding isn't quite what we'd recommend."

They all laughed, and even Trinity sniggered, Cordell noticed. *Good.*

"I'll have you know that wasn't my fault, young man," Frank admonished, playfully.

Jarrod turned to face him. "What? Surely, you're not blaming that poor horse, Frank?"

Cordell glanced over to see the fake expression of shock on Jarrod's face as his buddy put his hands on his cheeks.

Trinity giggled. It was quiet, but it was definitely a giggle.

"That's not what I said and you know it," Frank protested with a tut. He was clearly well-used to Jarrod's teasing.

"Sounded that way to me. What do you think, Trinity?" Jarrod goaded.

"I'm not getting involved," she told him. "I wasn't there, remember?"

"None of us were," Cordell offered, still watching her in the mirror. "In fact, we've got our suspicions that there wasn't even a horse involved at all. Seems to us your Uncle Frank might have had a little too much of his elderflower wine and simply fell over his own feet or something."

Jarrod hooted with laughter, and Cordell was pleased to see Trinity snigger, too. Her face seemed a little more relaxed now, and she was even more beautiful.

"That's a load of baloney and you know it," Frank protested, shaking his head. He was in his seventies, very well-dressed and had an authoritative air about him. Luckily, he also had a keen sense of humor.

"Oh, Frank, you know the guys are only kidding," Sylvia soothed him with a smile. She turned to Trinity. "They do this all the time, hon. You'll soon get used to it."

Trinity smiled, and Cordell noticed her glance up at him in the mirror then blush as she quickly turned away, obviously seeing that he was watching her. He grinned. She was a hard one to figure out. Her bright pink hair and nails gave the impression of a girl who oozed confidence, although she seemed anything but right now. He hoped that spending some time in Cavern County would help her recover from her ordeal and get back to her normal self—whatever that might be.

"Here we are," Frank announced as they pulled up on the drive outside his large house. "Let's get you inside, young lady. You must be worn out."

"No, I'm fine, honestly, Uncle Frank. I slept on the train," Trinity said.

Jarrod was already waiting to help Sylvia and Trinity out of the car so Cordell slowly made his way toward the house where Frank was unlocking the front door.

"I don't like it," the older man whispered. "I know she's just lost her home, but I reckon there's more to it than that. She used to be so bubbly and lively. Hell, it was hard to get a word in edgeways last time she was here. I'm gonna get to the bottom of all this if it kills me." His face tightened as he spoke.

Cordell frowned, but, noticing the women catching up to them, said nothing.

"I'll put the coffee on," Frank offered as they all piled into the hallway. It was a beautiful home, with high ceilings and large rooms.

"Let me show you your room," Sylvia told Trinity with a smile. She led her up the stairs while the guys went through to the kitchen.

"Where have you been hiding her?" Jarrod asked, hoisting himself up to sit on the counter. His long legs dangled and he rolled up the sleeves of his white cotton shirt to reveal his ripped arms.

"I told you. She lives in Nebraska," Frank told him gruffly. "She used to come out here for holidays and stuff when she was growing up, but since she's started working, we've hardly seen her."

"She's sure grown into a gorgeous woman," Jarrod remarked.

Cordell was expecting Frank to berate Jarrod, but instead, the old man frowned thoughtfully. "She has." He nodded.

"But she's got a boyfriend, right? I noticed she's wearing a ring with a heart on it."

Cordell stared pointedly at Jarrod, recalling how Frank had filled them in on the situation earlier. "Here, let me help." He took out the coffee cups and pointed to a high stool where Frank obediently plunked himself down with a sigh.

"That ring was her momma's. It's probably the only thing she's got left of her now." He pursed his lips. "She did have a boyfriend, though. I presume they're still together."

"Then where the hell is he?" Jarrod fumed. "He should be with her right now, not leaving her to deal with all this by herself. What sort of a man is he?"

Frank shook his head. "I never met him."

"Maybe that's part of the problem," Cordell offered. "If it was a bad split, it could have left her in a state, without her home going up in flames on top of it all. I think we need to tread carefully for a while, at least until we know the situation." He gave Jarrod one of his *I hope you're listening to this* stares before resuming preparation of the drinks.

He could feel Jarrod staring at the back of his head and knew his buddy had gotten his message loud and clear, although Cordell realized Jarrod wouldn't like it. Despite being one of the biggest flirts in Cavern County, Jarrod had a heart of gold. Cordell could see he liked Trinity — who wouldn't? — but he would need to tread carefully to avoid upsetting her. Jarrod's stunning appearance never failed to turn women weak at the knees, but in Trinity's case, that was the last thing she needed. The poor girl looked weak enough already.

He'd noted that Jarrod listened intently when Frank had told them last night that he would need a helping hand today, and he guessed the old man wasn't just referring to physical help. The poor guy had turned pale when he had explained to them that his niece had recently lost her home when a gas pipe exploded right outside her apartment building. Sylvia's sister — Trinity's mom — had passed away a few years ago, and the girl's dad hadn't been on the scene for a long while before that. Frank and Sylvia were worried sick about their niece and had insisted that she come to stay with them for a while. They were determined to care for her whether she wanted them to or not. She was quite independent, apparently, so had been a little reluctant to take them up on their offer.

About the Author

Bella Settarra is a British Erotic Romance author and lives in the beautiful English countryside.

She has several published novels to date, with subject matter including cowboys, BDSM and Myth/Fantasy. She has also written short stories for anthologies and has even had some raunchy poems published.

She likes to keep busy, cramming as much into each day as she possibly can, while battling—and is determined to win—against breast cancer. She loves to hear from her readers, so please get in touch!

Bella loves to hear from readers. You can find her contact information, website details and author profile page at http://www.totallybound.com.

Home of Erotic Romance